FAERIE CONFLUENCE

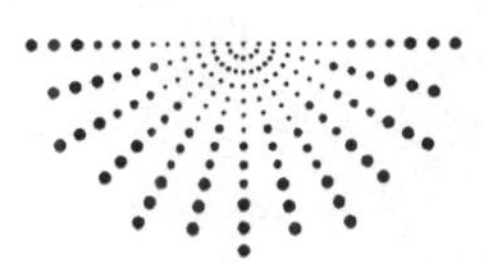

Fiachna breathed deeply. The place smelled of earth. The solidness of stones. He could still hear the thunder booming outside, but it was muffled.

He sat, catching his breath. The heat of his body, warmed from running, made his wet clothes steam. He felt tired and drained.

This war. He was sick of it. It accomplished nothing, but wasting lives.

They fought the Fomorians to no end. They had little effect on the giants. And in between fighting, they sat around waiting. Endless waiting.

And Clare's life was draining away. Humans didn't live even half as long as Fae. And her life was passing without him. He just wanted to spend the time she had left, with her.

What he did here, in this war, accomplished nothing.

He'd long given up hope that the Fae could win this war.

There had to be another solution.

Trouble was he didn't know what it was, and neither did anyone else.

FAERIE CONFLUENCE

THE BONES OF THE EARTH: BOOK 5

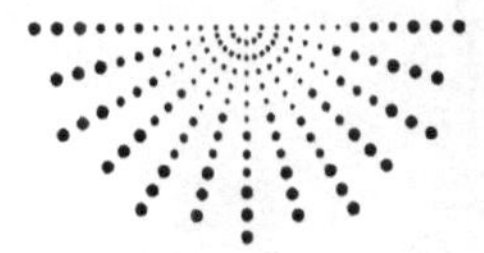

LINDA JORDAN

METAMORPHOSIS PRESS

Published by Metamorphosis Press

www.MetamorphosisPress.com

ISBN 13: 978-1946914026

For Michael & Zoe

CHAPTER 1 - FIACHNA

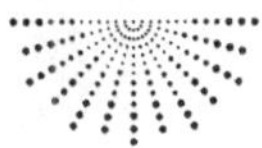

FIACHNA CROUCHED DEEP IN THE MEADOW GRASS. THE broken and bleached strands provided scant cover, only coming up to his chest. His sword sheath scraped on the limestone, which the grass grew up out of. He could feel Egan's hot breath on his back.

His mouth felt dry. Picking up a small broken piece of stone, he stuck it it his mouth. That helped. And not just because he was stone Fae.

Liquid trickled down his cheek. He wiped it off with the back of his hand and saw blood. He'd been hit by flying debris coming from the Fomorians' huge winds. The wound would heal, but leave a mark. He had never been among the best looking Fae. He hoped Clare wouldn't mind the scar.

His leather pants, boots, wool shirt and cloak were soaked through. His waist-length gray and brown hair was tied back. Driving rain streamed down his face. He ignored the discomfort. After spending millennia walking the boundaries of Faerie, this was nothing.

They hid downwind of the Fomorians. Watching and waiting. Crouched outside the boundary of Faerie.

The giants stank of rotted meat and their own filth. It had

been at least a month since they'd been released from the vault and even the near constant rain hadn't improved their smell.

The Fomorians had gathered with their offspring on the north side of Faerie. Fiachna couldn't actually see many of the winds, just their effect on the trees bordering the other side of the meadow. He felt freezing cold on his left, that must be Conand of the north wind. Humid heat on his right, might have been Hurricane. Surely, Domnu of the deep abyss of the ocean, wasn't there. She rarely came on land. Fiachna couldn't be sure who else was missing.

He certainly didn't underestimate them. They'd battled the Fae and dragons to a standstill. The Fomorians might be fewer, but Faerie still hadn't found a way to match their power.

He shifted his weight gradually, trying again to accurately count the moving enemy. So far the count was thirty-nine. He didn't recognize all of them.

Domnu, the Mother of them all, that great all-encompassing wave of ocean, scared him the most. He didn't see her and hoped she'd grown weary and gone home. Back to the depths.

Fiachna saw Cethlenn who resembled a flowing white vapor, like the fog she controlled. Corb of the sea, his watery body moving fluidly across the land. Conand of the north wind, taking the shape of a whirling gray and white mass. Elatha the great huntress, looking fierce with a necklace of bones. Dela, whose power he couldn't discern, but whose strong potent force was palpable.

Most of the Fomorians were always shifting. Continuously moving from a form that had two legs, two arms, a torso and a head, then back into their elemental body. Each one of those different from any other.

The rest of the Fomorians were offspring. Àed, the volcano, gray with red smoking depths. Muir of the deep black sea, with a body that couldn't seem to hold a shape. Ùisdean of the stone islands, with a gray angular body that even Fiachna of the stone people wouldn't want to go up against. There were also Fomorians whose powers looked like sea monsters, lightening and blizzards. Another one, so deep a black it looked like a hole in the world, stood off to the side. Saying nothing and not interacting with the others. That one had an ominous presence which set Fiachna on edge. Plague was the only name that came to mind.

Balor, the King of the Fomorians, sat on a boulder the size of a huge auroch. The giant was about twelve feet tall. Bellowing at all the others. His power was the ravage of drought. He had a third eye in the middle of his forehead which he'd covered with several pieces of cloth, one layered over the other, and tied in back. His baleful eye was a weapon that Fiachna hoped never to see again. He was one of the few Fomorians who Fiachna had never seen change form.

Balor stood up, looking at something near the boundary of Faerie.

Fiachna straightened up a bit, following the giant's gaze.

A cart was coming out of Faerie. Being pulled by a horse and accompanied by two Fae. Fiachna could feel the intense magic surrounding the cart.

Balor walked across the meadow towards it, the others following.

At their approach the illusionary Fae shrieked and ran back into Faerie. The horse, also not real, broke loose of its harness and headed back to Faerie as well. The magic was there for the Fomorian's benefit. Fiachna hoped they couldn't see through it.

The cart sat there, loaded down with bottles of mead as if on its way to a human village. As if it was normal for Fae to trade with humans.

"It's a trick," said Conand, as Balor picked up one of the bottles and uncorked it. The bottle looked like a child's glass in an adult's hand.

"Taste it," roared Balor, holding the bottle out.

The offspring exchanged glances, as if they didn't want to

obey and were waiting for one of the others to go first. Finally Muir, of the deep black sea, took it and sipped it.

"Take a big drink," said Balor.

Muir did. He handed the bottle back to Balor.

"What is it?" asked Elatha.

"It's mead."

"It has to be a trick. If it's not poisoned, then it must be enchanted," said Conand.

They all stared at the bottles and then at Muir, who was still licking his lips lips and smiling.

Nothing happened.

Then the all black one, Plague, spotted Fiachna and Egan.

Plague yelled, pointing with his arm, hand and finger, creating a dark line across the land.

Fiachna created a spell of confusion, and twisting, threw himself over Egan. He shifted completely into his element, earth. Turning into a large rock. Hard, whitish gray with moss attached in places.

He breathed heavily, shooting up a spell that might hide all the magic circling around them. Egan didn't move, just lay there, shutting his fire down.

Fiachna felt the ground shaking beneath him as the Fomorians came closer.

"What is it?"

"It's just a bloody rock," said Balor, kicking Fiachna in the ribs.

He didn't flinch, although pain shot through him.

"I saw something, I tell you," said Plague. "And it weren't no rock."

"Well I don't think the fucking Faeries can turn into boulders. Can they?" asked Corb.

"Nah," said one of the others, whose voice Fiachna didn't recognize.

"I wouldn't be so sure," said Dela. "They're tricky bastards those Fae."

"It's a rock," said Balor. "I hate this place."

"Gives me the creeps," said another.

"Let's leave," said a deeper voice.

"No!" roared Balor. "We leave when I say so. We get our revenge first."

"Then let's go drink some mead," said Plague.

Cethlenn said, "It's a trick. We can't eat or drink anything connected with Faerie."

"Then what good is it for us to knock all their walls down and take over? When we conquer it and can't eat or drink nuthin' then it's pointless," said a whiny voice.

"We conquer them, kill them all and destroy Faerie. Then we can leave," said Balor, as if tired of all the arguing.

Fiachna's belly felt far too warm. Egan wasn't holding his fire in well enough. If he didn't cool off Fiachna would begin to melt. He felt the spell keeping the magic invisible begin to waver. He was tired. Fiachna refocused his concentration.

"Let's try another area," said Dela. "Maybe their defenses aren't so strong where they haven't already been fighting."

The vibrations of their footsteps diminished into the distance.

Fiachna created a glamour that would disguise them and let go of the rock spell. A wave of fatigue ran through him as he opened his eyes. He couldn't see anyone, but the stink of Fomorians hung in the air. Was one of them hiding nearby?

He sent to Egan, *I think there's still one here. Stay still.*

They didn't move for a very long time. And even then, Fiachna kept the glamour of the large boulder lying in the middle of the meadow. As he and Egan melted back through the boundary of Faerie, Fiachna saw Plague standing at the other edge of the meadow, blending in with the dark tree trunks.

His eyes were glued to the boulder. Still watching.

Fomorians usually weren't that patient. This one they would need to be careful of.

Fiachna stood inside the transparent boundary, still invisible, keeping the glamour of the stone present.

Plague finally moved after the sun lowered behind the trees. In the growing dusk, Fiachna watched him move across the meadow and touch the stone. The Fomorian realized it wasn't real and stomped where the stone would have been.

Then Plague walked across the meadow to the boundary. He hit it and bounced backwards, repelled by the magic, unable to pass. The Fomorian tried to move very slowly through it, but the boundary pushed back, not allowing him in. He hit it hard and the boundary became as a thick metal wall. Impassable.

Fiachna used his magic to remain invisible and he could see through the boundary.

The Plague seemed more intelligent than most of the other Fomorians. One of the offspring, half Fomorian, half Fae. He should be watched carefully.

Finally, the Plague must have decided it was not worth his time. He turned and ran slowly off towards the east, following the others.

Fiachna let go of his invisibility once the giant was out of sight. Someone should probably go get the cart of mead.

But he turned and headed back to the palace. Let them decide what to do.

He felt tired, unused to doing this kind of magic for such a long time.

He was tired of war.

Fiachna just wanted to return to Glastonbury.

And Clare.

CHAPTER 2 - EGAN

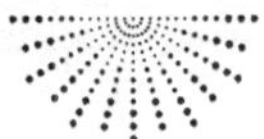

EGAN STOOD IN FRONT OF THE COUNCIL OF LUMINARIES, waiting for the Fae ahead of him to finish. The Council sat in their chairs in the throne room of the palace. It had changed since he'd stepped down as Luminary. Relieved of a great burden.

What had once been stone pillars were now the living trunks of grand trees. The walls were formed of willows, also alive and woven so close together by the palace that even air couldn't flow between them. On some of the walls colorful tapestries attached themselves to the willows.

The throne room was nearly empty of Fae at this time of day, just the Council and a few others.

Light streamed in through huge windows of colored glass pieced together in intricate designs of plants and animals, making a rainbow of colors on the floor and faces.

Egan poured a cup of hot black tea from a teapot sitting on a nearby table. He sipped it, replenishing some of his own lost liquid. He longed for a cup of coffee. He'd acquired a taste for it while living in the human world and owning a restaurant. The earth spirits in the kitchen just shook their heads and looked confused when he'd once mentioned they might want to acquire coffee beans and try making some.

Between the fire at his back and his own heat, the wet leather clothes he wore had begun to steam. It actually felt quite pleasant.

He looked forward to reporting in and then going to find a warm fire, like the one behind him, to sleep in.

Conley caught his eye and nodded at Egan, understanding his hurry.

The fire elder sat on a chair made of silver, gold and black metal forged to create the shape of dancing flames. Like all fire Fae he was hairless. His head, back, chest and arms scaled in red, orange and yellow. His eyes yellow with black pupils.

The water elder, Meredith had a wooden chair carved with designs of sea creatures, and a woven blue and green blanket draped over over the edge it. The blanket was probably made of something that repelled liquids as water Fae normally oozed water. She sat looking outward with her clear, blue-green eyes. Her skin was sea green. Meredith's long, long, hair looked as if someone had put a living creature on top of her head. It moved as if it had a will of its own.

Alana, the stone elder, sat on a chair that looked like blocks of stacked limestone. Very simple, rugged and utilitarian. She looked like part of the chair with her chiseled features and gray skin, steely gray eyes and waist-length hair the same color.

Ogden, an ancient dryad, had a beard that looked like dried moss and gnarled bark. He sat on a chair made of a solid looking, living tree, which formed one of the pillars of the palace, a double trunked oak. One trunk shot straight upwards, the other twisted and curved to form a seat, back and armrests. The leaves were just beginning to turn scarlet, a signal that fall was in full swing. A dark green cushion sat on the seat.

Brian, another earth elder, had a wooden chair carved with a mountain scene covered with grasses and flowers. He stood next to his chair, tall with long, wispy hair. His face, soft and peaceful, open as a grassy meadow.

Aura, the air elder, had a tall, fanciful chair made of branches tied together with blue, purple and silver fabric. A transparent silver veil was woven through the branches. It matched the color and gossamer-like quality of her wings perfectly. Her delicate features were outlined by her ankle-length silver hair.

The palace had done an extraordinary job in creating these chairs, each one capturing the essence of its intended inhabitant. As it did with the entire palace. Reflecting what Faerie needed at the time. It felt balanced.

He'd seen the palace under three other Luminaries. The first one had been a water Fae, the one who'd originally closed Faerie against human contact. Egan, and many other Fae, had disagreed with the action. And they'd left.

The palace then had been domed with an opalescent sheen. It had left like walking underwater every time he entered it. Entirely uncomfortable for a fire Fae. He hadn't been sorry to leave Faerie then.

When he'd returned to warn Faerie of the invading Fomorians, Varion had been Luminary. An earth Fae born from a dryad mother and a water sprite father, he'd been a weak and ineffective leader. The palace had been a tangle of brush, stuffy and unkempt.

And when Egan, himself, had been Luminary, the palace had been all metal and stone. Filled with fire everywhere. He'd alienated all the earth and water elementals. Except for the stone people. They could handle the heat. Egan had been relieved to have the Council step in and take over. He had just wanted to save Faerie. Not to rule.

It had cost him too much.

He thought sadly of Lassair, gone back to her village, with her daughter, to work her pepper magic there. She'd hated the palace and living inside. But mostly, she'd hated that he could never be with her. She was used to living in the woods, surrounded by family and friends, and healing them. Not worrying about the affairs of the larger world, like Fomorians and humans.

And he'd just watched her go. Hurt, and overwhelmed with trying to hold Faerie together.

Egan sipped the hot tea again. Reveling in the flavor of fermented, steeped camellia leaves. He breathed in its warmth.

Now, the palace was a thing of beauty. All Fae were represented and welcome here. The Council had been a perfect idea. The elders were meant to rule. They had the knowledge and power that he did not. Together they formed a balance that no one Fae could equal.

The Fae in front of him bowed and left the circle.

Egan stepped forward and bowed at the elders.

"Well Egan, what happened with the mead?" asked Meredith.

"One of them drank some, to test it. Then, they were distracted. They spotted us. We hid, Fiachna turned into a stone. But they decided the mead was a trap. Cethlenn warned them never to eat or drink anything Fae left for them. That it might be enchanted."

Meredith sank back into her chair.

Brian said, "Well, it was worth a try. It tamed them once before."

Aura's face drooped with disappointment.

Alana asked, "Where is Fiachna?"

"He went to dry off and sleep," said Egan. "He'd been awake for days."

Alana nodded and sat back against the stone behind her.

"We will just have to come up with another idea," said Aura.

"We have already tried a dozen different things," said Conley. "Nothing has worked."

"Well, we cannot give up," said Aura. "We cannot give up the defense of Faerie."

"You are right of course," said Conley. "I simply have no more ideas."

"I'll go back down to the library," sighed Meredith.

"No," said Aura. "I'll go. You go swim. I went flying this morning, with the other sylphs, and it was invigorating. We all need to get out of the palace and spend time in our elements."

Meredith said, "Good advice. I think I'll go down to the lake."

Conley said to Egan, "You can go. I will call if you are needed."

Egan nodded. He drained the tea from his mug and set it down on a table near the door on his way out of the room.

The windows in the entryway revealed it was still drizzling. His leather clothes and wool cloak had mostly dried. He left the cloak in the entryway where outdoor clothes were apparently being kept these days, judging by the neatly folded piles of sweaters and coats, and the row of boots.

Then Egan went outside and down the stone stairs. Past the vault, now scoured clean but closed and empty. It had recently been a prison for the Fomorians. He'd been a part of that. Before that, the vault had housed the treasures of Faerie. Most of them ruined by the Fomorian's filth, and burned as a result.

His heart sank every time he walked by the vault.

His life felt ruined.

Faerie was embroiled in an unwinnable war. Countless lives had been lost. Fae, not Fomorian. His own life was a mess. He often considered whether to leave Faerie, make another human body and go hide in the human world again. He'd been content in Santa Fe. Mostly.

But was content enough?

He felt depressed. Who wouldn't, under the circumstances?

Egan continued down the wide stone steps beside the palace. Down in the plaza a huge oil fire blazed. Stoked with the bodies of fire Fae. He removed his boots and lay them sideways so they wouldn't collect rainwater. Then removed his clothes and hung them on an iron rack, along with those of other fire Fae.

He stood naked in the rain, the water making his black, red, yellow and orange scales shine brighter. They covered the top of his head and forehead, back, shoulders and the tops of his arms. Lately, he'd been growing scales on the tops of his feet too. Scale growth usually meant an increase in power, but he couldn't feel it.

He sighed and stepped into the purifying fire, joining the other fire spirits.

The heat cleansed him, warming his body slightly. It would take hours before he was fully warm again.

Egan moved through the flames, finding an empty spot and sat down, feeling the red heat move through him. He opened himself to the fire, letting it into every space in his body. Feeling ease and contentment flow through him.

Making him wonder why he ever left the fire.

CHAPTER 3 - SPIKE

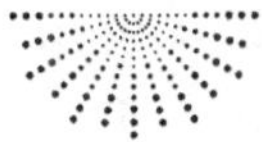

Spike sat just outside the first ring of the circle, straining to hear what the wise ones were saying tonight, as he did every night. The cave floor felt warm where he'd been sitting, but cold when he swished his tail over a new spot. The fire in this room of the caves had died down.

The wise ones were talking about the war on the Fomorians. He'd been listening. He was too young and foolish to be part of the conversation, but interested all the same.

It was long past his time to sleep. He felt wide awake. Even though his belly bulged from his weekly fishing trip. Like most dragons he normally ate once a week, then slept for several days.

The room was crowded. It was one of the smaller rooms in the cave complex. The rock wall was covered with paintings done by dragons of generations long gone. Scenes of everyday life, as well as great events, like when Azure the Magnificent overcame the humans who invaded his land. The floor was inlaid with precious stones to form a complex design. These made the room gleam golden, blue, green and red in the firelight.

The dragons formed part of that rainbow of colors. Spike admired the colors of their shiny scales. He was an ordinary, coal black with dull scales. Black dragons had only recently been forgiven for their ancestors' sins. He still felt like an outcast and wished he'd been born different. Anything but black, and an ugly, dull black at that.

Attania was the color of sapphires. Goshania, emeralds. Keirosum, rubies and sunset-red shiny scales. Silver glistened like the metal she was named for. Ethelgarde was a flashing rainbow of precious opals. Maximus, the color of pure gold.

"I do not see how we can help them any more," said Maximus, fluttering his massive wings. "Our efforts have been ineffective, and now we have hatchings to protect."

"But if Faerie falls, then so do we," said Goshania, her emerald tail slapping the floor as an added exclamation.

"She is right," said Ethelgarde, who spoke rarely. "We are part of Faerie again. If we do not help, it will be seen as an insult. We cannot afford to insult the Fae again."

"I personally, am benefitting greatly from learning their magic," said Attania, her tail thumping on the floor.

"What do you think Spike?" asked Silver, the eldest of them all. She scratched her chest with a front claw.

Spike backed up in surprise. He felt caught out.

"I am too young to have an opinion," he said.

"Nonsense," said Marusa, the color of amethyst. "You are one of those closest to the Fae, carrying Dylan around so much."

"I do not know what will insult the Fae. But I feel a … duty to them. They have forgiven black dragons for the murders we began. They requested that everyone forgive us, allowed us to be named again. For that alone, I owe them. But beyond that, they have begun to teach us their magic. And allowed us to return to our caves in the protection of Faerie again. Within their magic I feel safer, less hungry and more powerful. I cannot speak for anyone else."

"Those are wise words, especially coming from one so young," said Silver. "Thank you."

With that, the first row stepped aside and invited him in.

Hesitantly, he stepped forward, closer to the fire. The spikes around his neck twitched with excitement. He shook his head as if to clear his ears, unwilling to betray his feelings.

"I believe we should follow their lead," said Keirosum. "Wait for the Fae to decide what to do next. Their libraries are vast, as is their magic. We have no experience with the Fomorians. We have exhausted our magic fighting them, as Maximus said, to little effect."

"We need to send a message to them. To let them know we are waiting to help, if only they will tell us how," said Silver. "I believe we should concentrate on teaching the hatchlings and on deepening the caves here. The hatchlings learning is underway, but who shall we put in charge of digging?"

Iru, the color of fiery topaz, said, "Carbon. He has a good sense of the structure of these mountains."

"I agree," said Goshania.

"Who will go speak to the Fae?" asked Silver.

"I would be honored," said Spike.

The others all bobbed their heads in agreement.

"Should I go tonight?"

"No let them sleep," said Silver. "Tomorrow is soon enough."

Spike bowed his head in acknowledgement.

The conversation moved to a discussion of how to integrate Fae magic with that of dragons.

Attania said, "The main problem is that the Fae divide up their magical abilities strangely. With dragon magic, most of us will be able to do everything the others can, given time and an accumulation of power. With Fae, there is some common magic, but much of it is divided up by elements. Air Fae have different magic than the stone people. The fire Fae are vastly different than water elementals. Meredith has suggested that each of us try to learn from the various elders and see what works for us. She has found little in their library about dragons and Fae magic."

"Is she telling you everything she knows?" asked Iru.

"I believe she is," said Attania. "At least on that subject. There are spells she hasn't shared. Meredith has said that with her students she begins with the basics. Once those are mastered, then she will teach the next level."

"I truly don't understand Fae," said Maximus.

Spike swished the tip of his tail in annoyance. Maximus always irritated him. With Maximus there was only his way of thinking. Everyone else was wrong.

Behind him, Spike heard a squealing sound. And the thud of a heavy dragon.

He turned to see a hatchling burst into the cavern followed by one of the minders. He didn't recognize the minder, a large fuchsia colored dragon with ruffles around her neck. The hatchling was yellow and black scaled. It stopped quickly as all heads turned its way.

Then it ran into Ethelgarde, easily the largest dragon in the cave. The hatchling tumbled end over end and righted itself. Ethelgarde bent his long neck so he was nose to nose with the hatchling. He sniffed it and the little one squealed again. Then moved backwards away from the large dragon.

"Come here you," said the minder, who was very attractive indeed. "You cannot be bothering the wise ones. They have important things to decide and you are a distraction."

She scuttled the little one out of the cave, but not before meeting Spike's eyes, giving him a look that made the protrusions on his neck stand up just a little bit straighter with pride, at being included with the wise ones.

Eventually, the talk wound down. Some of the wise ones stayed, sleeping by the fire. Iru fed the fire with a pile of wood that had been collected earlier in the day. The rest went off to seek other sleeping places.

Spike curled up by the fire, unwilling to leave the circle until he had to in the morning. The hard stone floor wasn't where he normally slept. Usually, he sought out a bed made from soft, meadow grasses in a nook of the largest cavern. Where most of those his age slept after playing flying games all evening.

But tonight he would sleep here. With the wise ones. He was growing up. Finally.

He dreamt of the fuchsia dragon. Just the two of them, necks entwined watching the magic of the returning sun.

CHAPTER 4 - SOLANGE

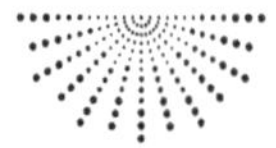

SOLANGE SAT ON THE LUMPY, DOWN-FILLED MATTRESS. IT needed to be given a good thumping and dried out again. It was damp, even with a waterproof mattress pad. Dylan had spent a lot of time on it last night and his skin leaked everywhere.

She watched him standing in front of the easel, naked. Looking at a watercolor he was working on. Or rather, not working on. He'd gotten the bluish-green background done days ago and then walked away from it. What did he see? It was just a wash of color. Nothing else.

She crossed her legs and pulled the silky sheet over her bare legs and torso, the coolness of the room chilling her. She should get dressed and go downstairs to eat. Her belly growled and she was thirsty. Unlike the Fae, she needed to eat and drink on a regular basis.

But she didn't want to get up. Her body didn't really want to move.

Faerie had made her lazy.

She'd spent her early years in a whirlwind of school, ballet, soccer, violin lessons, volunteering at the food bank, then at an animal shelter. After college she'd worked as a freelance photographer, spending her time in airport after airport, plane after plane, hiking up mountains and down canyons. Specializing in wildlife photos. And pushing, pushing, always pushing to sell the next photo. And mostly, making ends meet. But it felt like she'd been hustling her entire life. Her friends and family had drifted away. Or maybe she had. Their routine, happy lives so different from hers. Until they no longer shared much of anything.

Then she met Dylan, three years ago.

She'd fallen in love with his long, grassy hair, greenish skin, muscular body and those deep eyes. And lost her soul, or maybe found it.

Even his laugh delighted her.

It had taken her months of being alone in the human world before she decided to give it all up and come to Faerie for good. Walking away from the life she'd struggled so hard to create. Faerie had felt like home. Even if she wasn't Fae and had no magic. She loved him and this place.

Even if he exasperated her.

Like now.

Solange suddenly felt hot and pushed the sheet away. She should just get up and get dressed. Go eat. She didn't want to argue about him avoiding painting any more.

After breakfast, she'd go down to the library. See if she could help unearth the miracle that Meredith and Aura were searching for in the ancient collection of Faerie's wisdom.

Solange loved the smell of that room. Old paper, or maybe it was the glue, or the leather. And the palace always kept the fireplace in the library well stoked, so the manuscripts wouldn't mildew and decay. The room always felt, warm, welcoming and cosy. She loved spreading an old manuscript on the table and trying to decipher it in the warm light the oil lamps gave off.

It was a sanctuary where she could use her skill of tenacity. Meredith had taught her how to read the old language. Once she'd mastered that, Solange learned so much. Things even Fae had long forgotten. Just as they'd forgotten about the library. For millennia.

She slid off the bed and went to the wardrobe. Pulling out loose tan cotton pants from a drawer, she slipped them on. Fae didn't make underwear, and after washing the ones she'd brought with her from home, dozens of times, they'd fallen apart and she'd just given up wearing them altogether. Solange put on a loose-fitting, sky blue blouse. And slipped her feet into wool clogs.

In front of a mirror, she pulled a brush through her tangled hair. It now reached the middle of her back. Short for Faerie. Many Fae had knee or even ankle length hair. She tied her hair back with a strip of leather. She had things to do and hated having to deal with her hair while working.

Dylan was still staring at the painting.

Solange walked up to him and kissed his wet cheek. Water Fae were always wet. If they were healthy, at least.

He didn't look at her.

"Call for Spike. He needs you," she said. "And get back to painting. Do the work you need to be doing. Teaching young water Fae is not feeding you."

She walked out of the room.

CHAPTER 5 - LEA

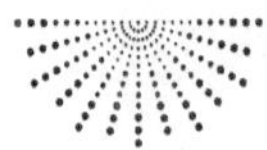

Lea walked through the oak forest with Bryan and Ogden. She could feel the change in the air, even without smelling it. The breeze that swirled around her felt crisp this morning. She could feel it even through the deerskin leggings and shirt. And the leather shoes she wore crunched the leaves beneath her feet. Her golden yellow and silver hair tangled and untangled itself around her ankles with each step, as if playing a game. Her skin, once again the color of dried grass and her eyes copper. She struggled with the long process of remembering herself after having been magicked into a fox for so many years. It was a struggle to not get on her hands and sniff at the underbrush.

The rains had let up enough so that the newly fallen leaves weren't a sodden mass. The forest floor was littered with yellows, oranges, a bit of red, golden and dark browns. The surrounding live trees still carried some leaves which covered them like a glorious cloak. The smell of the leaves filled her nostrils, even more keen from spending several seasons as a fox.

The Fomorians had caught her and obviously enjoyed bespelling her. She'd escaped from them and wandered through Faerie for a very long time, confused and lost, as a fox. She'd been unable to make herself understood until she'd happened onto the right place at the right time. The other elders had broken the spell, returning her to herself.

But much changed.

Lea couldn't tell how much time she'd passed in fox form. The seasons had come and passed. She'd hunted, slept and hunted again. Throughout leaf drop, snow, flowers, heat and leaf drop again. Her mind had grown more focused only on survival as each season passed.

Until she met the dryad, Adaire. Who reminded Lea of who and what she really was.

And saved her sanity.

Today, Brian, Ogden and Lea were walking part of the northern boundary of Faerie. Looking at the damage done to plants and trying to see what needed to be done over the winter to help them thrive come spring.

This section was filled with burnt and blasted trees. Charred trunks still standing as monuments to the war between Fae and Fomorian. They would eventually make nice homes for bats and other birds. But right now, they stood out and looked ugly.

Ogden said, "Once the rains are truly come, I will send a group of dryads here to plant more trees."

Lea looked up at a massive unscathed holly tree that grew on the edge of the burnt area. She recognized the tree and looked back at the burnt out area.

"I recognize this place. When I was a child, this was all meadow. Filled with spotted orchids, ragged robins, dog roses and self-heal. It was beautiful. Beloved by the deer and birds. So many healing herbs grew here," she said.

Bryan said, "And then it was taken over by a forest, wasn't it? Well, our meadows are dwindling, being shaded out. Perhaps we should help this place return to meadow again. We need to be in balance."

Lea looked at Ogden. He nodded in affirmation.

She said, "I will bring some others here this fall with roots and seeds to get started. And we will take down some of these dead trunks. Leave others up for birds. Come spring it will be a glorious, life filled place again."

She could see it in her mind. The yellows, pinks and white of the majority of wildflowers. There must still be stones beneath all the debris, where the hardiest of wildflowers could take hold.

Ogden said, "You know Lea, the Council of Luminaries is open to all elders."

"And do you actually think I would be of most use sitting in the throne room, making decisions?"

"You have some firsthand knowledge of the Fomorians. Most of us do not."

Lea sighed and said, "I told you everything that happened. All I know of them. I really do not think I would be useful making decisions. Not when there is other work I could be doing."

"What about teaching?" asked Ogden.

"I could do that. Send some of those who want to learn more plant magic with me to help restore this meadow. I'll teach them what I know."

Just then a giant shadow moved across the land. Lea looked up to see a dragon. She immediately crouched next to a burned tree stump, casting a veil of invisibility over herself. Her heart pounding with fear.

It took her some time before she dared to breathe again.

Brian and Ogden, the fools, just stood out in the open staring at the dragon. After it had passed they looked around, unable to find her. Her spell was that perfect.

Then it struck her why they weren't afraid. She'd forgotten Faerie was open to the dragons. And that somehow dragons and Fae were friends. She'd spent her entire life seeing dragons as the most threatening creature that ever lived.

Old habits die hard.

She dropped the veil of invisibility and stood.

"Oh, there you are," said Brian.

"I forgot. About the dragons."

"You know that we teach them our magic," said Ogden.

"I heard."

"Would you be willing to share what you know with them?" asked Brian.

"Why would they want to know plant magic?"

"I do not know," Brian said. "I believe they simply love to learn. But they would be very helpful to clear this land of some of the dead trees. Being around one might help you be less afraid."

She doubted that. Even as a fox she'd felt they were to be feared.

Was it possible she'd been wrong?

CHAPTER 6 - SKYE

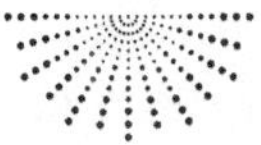

SKYE CIRCLED JUST BEHIND THE GROVE OF ROWAN TREES AT the western boundary of Faerie. She flew through the canopy of their brilliant red leaves and orangish berry clusters. That, and the spell she was using, kept her invisible to the group of Fomorians she was shadowing.

The air was colder here on her naked body. The wind made her long hair ripple even though she'd plaited it into one heavy braid. She was flying at the foot of a mountain. And the wind was blowing in from the north. She sensed it was a normal wind. The Fomorians hadn't yet found a way to enter into Faerie.

Especially the winds. Ever since they'd captured her over the Pacific Ocean, Skye had a particular horror of them.

Unfortunately, the wind blew their awful scent in her direction. A smell she could only describe as a mixture of rotted meat and shit. They didn't smell as bad as normal though. Which was a relief. The sound of gagging might give her away.

She watched this band of Fomorians. They had split off from the main group. There had been an argument. Nothing new. Fomorians always argued.

This group contained Ùisdean, Muir, who controlled some aspect of water and was the one she'd encountered in

Glastonbury, Hurricane, Lightning, Blizzard, Àed, who controlled volcanoes, and the solid black one Fiachna had warned her about. He'd dubbed that one Plague. There were several others she didn't recognize.

This band seemed to be all offspring. Their power felt different than the original Fomorians. She couldn't quite describe the difference. They were not as strong, but their magic seemed more deadly. They were smarter. Half Fomorian and half Fae. Or perhaps even more than half. She could feel a kinship even through the boundary.

And she knew they could do Fae magic, like transforming Lea into a fox. Could they also pass through the boundary?

No one had seen any sign that they could.

Then it occurred to her. If she could sense their Fae blood, could they sense hers?

The large one, who called himself Ùisdean, stomped his foot in anger. Much like a two year old.

Except that in response to his stomping the surrounding landscape shook, as if during an earthquake. The trees swayed. A couple boulders rolled down the mountainside behind her, making a crashing noise as they hit pines growing on the slope.

She flew to get out of their way.

He stomped again. The trees swayed more. One of the rowans, uprooted by the earth's movement, fell crashing against the others. Breaking one and forcing another to uproot itself and fall as well.

One of them blew and the trees swayed.

The Fomorians roared with laughter.

Skye was horrified.

The offspring could see through the boundary and into Faerie.

Skye felt grateful for Aura's advice that she always use the transparency spell.

The Fomorians stared, watching the trees fall. She could

almost feel them staring at her. How much magic did being part Fae grant one?

Could they see through her magic? She didn't have as much experience with the offspring as some of the stone and fire Fae. The ones who'd been fighting this war.

She felt more and more uncomfortable, even with hiding behind the trees. Skye could feel them throwing all their power in her direction. Finally, she turned and sped off.

Flying as fast as she could back to the palace.

She wasn't cut out for this. She was a healer, not a spy. And certainly not a warrior.

It was a long flight back to the palace. She'd been at the farthest edge of Faerie. The flight winded her. Since she'd returned from the human world in Glastonbury, Skye hadn't flown as much as she should have. Spending so much time in a human body had weakened her. She was terribly out of shape.

In her panic and trying to catch her breath, Skye nearly hit a pair of robins.

"Sorry," she called back at the poor shaken birds, squawking their way towards an oak tree.

She continued streaking through the forest, across meadows and sometimes following a road paved with large, flat gray stones. A couple of times she even passed through the gaps between mountains.

Skye landed on the road and sat on a boulder, breathing hard. She dropped the invisibility spell. Needed to save some energy somewhere. She really would try to get back in shape for flying, but that promise didn't help her now. She'd never been this badly out of shape in her life. Her wings felt limp. She couldn't raise them any more. She'd need to walk for a bit and let them rest.

Her rapid breathing was so loud, she barely heard a rustling in the bushes behind her. She stood looking, but saw nothing. Beneath the low canopy of oaks all was shadow. The sun had already dropped behind the trees and would set soon.

She walked for a bit, her wings drooping behind her. Breathing hard.

Then it began to rain. She should stand under an evergreen to keep dry. Wait out the storm. She sure couldn't fly well in this deluge. But who knew how long it would last? This was fall. It could rain for days.

She kept walking. Cold, wet, naked and barefoot. It was getting dark. None of this was helping.

For a moment, Skye wished she was back in Glastonbury. Tucked inside her warm, human body and helping someone heal. Or maybe sitting in a chip shop. Eating fish smothered with tartar. Or just hanging out at Clare's beautiful store.

Her belly began to growl with hunger.

"Stop. Just stop," she told herself.

"Stop what?" came a voice from behind her.

Skye whirled to see a large bulky shape on the road behind her.

It was the size of an elephant.

"Who are you?" she asked.

"I have no name yet," said the dark shape.

"What are you? I can't see you very well."

She used to be able to see in the dark. Sylphs can always see in the dark. What was wrong with her these days?

The creature stepped forward.

Closer now, she could make out the black and dark blue form. It was a small dragon, perhaps a baby. Not like the massive one she'd ridden back from England.

This one was sleek and streamlined with a narrow head and long slender neck. The large wings folded back. He only had four legs. The whiplike tail dragged on the ground behind him, probably about half as long as the creature's body.

"Where did you come from?" she asked.

"I was sitting on the edge of my cave. And I saw you streak past. I just flew after you and followed."

"Why?"

"Because it looked like fun. And you were fast. I wanted to see if I could fly as fast as you."

"Well, you probably should go back now. I'm sure someone's worried about you."

"I do not know where I am. I have not ever flown this far from the cave before."

Skye sighed. She didn't want to be responsible for taking care of anyone else, not now. She couldn't even take care of herself.

Her back and wings ached. She just wanted to curl up someplace warm and sleep, but she needed to get to the palace.

"Okay, you can follow me to the palace. We'll make sure you get back home."

"I do not know what home means, but I will joyfully follow you."

As they walked the dragon kept asking her the names of common things. Like what type of tree was that? Or stone? As they walked through a clearing he wanted to know what the stars were and could he fly to it.

Skye decided the dragon was very, very young. And curious. She'd heard the dragons' eggs were hatching and there was much rejoicing among them.

She felt exhausted. The dragon's questions and her own answers at least took her mind off of the aching that seemed to reach all the way down to her bones.

At one point, she stopped and looked around.

The half moon had risen and cast light on the road. She could see a beautiful stone sculpture standing beside the road. It was of the goddess Danu, carrying an armful of bounty: fruits, vegetables, vines of ripe berries. Gifts to her children, the Fae.

"I know where we are," said Skye. "If we keep following the road, we'll end up right at the palace. It's not far now."

The last thing she remembered was dropping to the ground.

CHAPTER 7 - FIACHNA

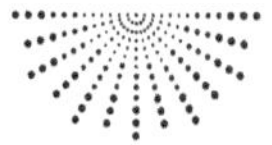

FIACHNA LED THE GROUP OF STONE WARRIORS OVER THE RISE.
He felt his own essence connect with the earth beneath his feet
with every single step. Like touching like. Even through his
heavy leather boots.

The hills in this area stood bare of trees. Covered with
heather and grasses, open to the sea beyond.

Exposed stone lay everywhere.

And just there over by the cliffs overlooking the sea, stood a
group of Fomorians.

He recognized Corb and Cethlenn. Balor must be nearby.
And Domnu.

Fiachna could smell the sea, all salt and kelp.

A fine mist touched his face, caressing it. If he hadn't been in
Faerie, he would have thought it was a Fomorian. But he *was* in
Faerie. And the boundaries were still up. They couldn't pass
through the boundary.

He didn't know what Alana had thought they could do about
the earthquakes, but he'd come out here anyway. It was better
than sitting around the throne room, waiting for something to
happen.

He knew what the cause was. The Fomorians. Or one of them. But he didn't see the one who usually caused earthquakes. Ùisdean. All of the offspring were missing. Only the original seven Fomorians stood there. Provided Domnu was here. He didn't want to find out.

He stopped the stone warriors. Pearce came up beside him, caught his eye and nodded at the Fomorians. Then looked back at Fiachna.

Fiachna nodded. *Yes, I see them.*

The stone Fae, instinctively, each chose a large boulder. Slid up near it and melded with the stone. Blending in without using much magic. Not enough for anyone to sense.

In the near darkness caused by the heavy, gray cloud cover, they were invisible.

Fiachna had blended into a large upright stone, not quite becoming stone, but anyone looking closely wouldn't have been able to see him. A remnant of something built by ancient humans. Mimicking the even more primordial barrows made by the stone Fae.

It still carried a resonance for him because of the powerful stones. The bones of the earth, they were.

The fine mist turned to a steady rain. Fiachna slowly turned his head upwards and caught some water to wet his mouth. The taste sweeter than any berry.

The rain became so heavy, he lost sight of the Fomorians, but he could still smell them. They hadn't disappeared. He could hear them too.

Balor was bellowing.

"I don't care about the youngsters. They're soft. They can leave. We don't need them."

Someone else, with a throaty, husky feminine voice was disagreeing with him. Not likely Cethlenn. Perhaps Elatha or Dela. He couldn't hear what she said though.

The rain pounded harder the rocks around him, creating more noise.

Fiachna strained to hear, but couldn't. Now the storm was creating too much noise.

He sent to the others, *"Stay put. We will wait the storm out. Nothing we can learn until then."*

Pearce sent to him, *"I can get closer."*

"No, we are not to risk being seen."

Fiachna slowly crouched down on the side of the stone that would give him the most protection from the battering wind and rain. Lightning flashed out over the sea and thunder followed close behind.

The next lightning strike was closer. The storm was moving this way. And it wasn't a natural storm.

He sent to the others, *"Retreat to the barrow we saw on the other side of the hill. Quickly."*

They detached themselves from the stones and fled back over the hill, running through the darkness punctuated by flashes of lightning. Hoping to remain unseen by the Fomorians.

Fiachna led the way to the grass covered barrow. He stood in front of it and drew power up from the stone beneath his feet. Then with a finger nudged the entry stone aside. He entered first, bending over to make his way through the short structure. Noting the emptiness even in the dark. This one had never been used as a burial mound.

The seven of them crammed into the cramped barrow. Out of the wind and rain at least. The stones above them would give them some protection from lightning. It was a fearsome storm.

Were the Fomorians immune to it? What would happen if their tall bodies drew the lightning? Probably nothing. They seemed impervious to everything, including dragon fire.

He sat with the seven others on the rocky limestone floor of the barrow. Clothes soaking, skin wet, water still streaming down his face from his hair. Pearce, the last one inside, pulled the heavy entry stone back over the door, shutting out the storm.

Even though they were still inside the boundaries of Faerie. All of them had been in this war long enough to be cautious.

Fiachna breathed deeply. The place smelled of earth. The solidness of stones. He could still hear the thunder booming outside, but it was muffled.

He sat, catching his breath. The heat of his body, warmed from running, made his wet clothes steam. He felt tired and drained.

This war. He was sick of it. It accomplished nothing, but wasting lives.

They fought the Fomorians to no end. They had little effect on the giants. And in between fighting, they sat around waiting. Endless waiting.

And Clare's life was draining away. Humans didn't live even half as long as Fae. And her life was passing without him. He just wanted to spend the time she had left, with her.

What he did here, in this war, accomplished nothing.

He'd long given up hope that the Fae could win this war.

There had to be another solution.

Trouble was he didn't know what it was, and neither did anyone else.

CHAPTER 8 - EGAN

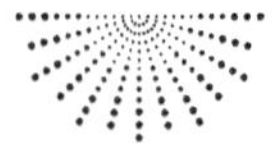

THREE DAYS PASSED BEFORE EGAN GAINED SOME CLARITY. HE slept in the raging fire. Then woke and stared into the center of the blue white flames. Feeling it heat him to the core.

Within the fire everything was clear.

The fire cleansed him of confusion. Maybe if was because the flames created such noise that they blocked out everything else.

There were at least eight other fire Fae in the flames. Only one was awake. Oiling herself. Which reminded him to do the same.

He moved into a part of the fire that was red and orange and sat down by a bronze oil pot.

He dipped his warm hands into the pot of hot oil and rubbed them over the new scales on the top of his feet. Letting the oil soften the scales a bit until they were flexible. The oil smelled slightly like scented flowers, but Egan couldn't have said what kind. Fire Fae didn't know much of anything about flowers or plants. They generally stayed away from them, so as not to cause harm. He poured some of the oil over his back, basking in the heat sliding down his scales. There was a soft wire brush with a long handle nearby. He took it and used it on his back, spreading the oil evenly.

The red and black scales of his arms and hands glistened in the intense light of the main fire. Warm and oiled, he felt invigorated.

When was the last time he'd spent this long in a fire? There had been too much to do since he'd returned to Faerie.

Egan was now one of the oldest fire Fae who was still conscious and active. The ancient elders were sleeping in the heart of fires. Possibly bathing in the magma of volcanoes. Unreachable. Here in Faerie, only Conley was older than he.

Egan had been spawned in a volcano. Fire spirits were among the most ancient Fae. When the Fomorians had stepped ashore, he'd still been young. When the dryads came into existence, he'd been there. He was older than Faerie herself. He remembered the time before and didn't want to return to that. The Fomorians wrought chaos wherever they went.

But in reality, there was nothing he could do concerning the Fomorians that other Fae couldn't do just as well. He'd used all his knowledge, skill and power against them. It had barely fazed the giants.

He was finished. With nothing more to give to this war. Or to Faerie.

It was time to rebuild his shattered life. And go find Lassair.

He should have followed her when she left. A love like theirs was a once, in a very long lifetime, event.

Perhaps it was already too late.

Egan reluctantly left the heat of the flames and the other sleeping and healing fire Fae.

It was cold outside. Winter was coming. He put on the now dry but stiff leather pants and shirt. Then slipped into his cold boots.

A wizened fire Fae was roasting a deer over a small cooking fire. Egan asked for and was given a chunk of the hot meat. In return he added a blast of his energy to keep the fire burning longer with less fuel. The old fire Fae bowed in thanks. Egan returned the bow and ate as he walked. The hot meat's succulent juices filled his senses with the taste of wildness.

He had been tame too long.

Egan ran through the woods on a dirt path that led down to the lake. He made good time. The cool wind whipped past his face and neck, but the fire inside him still burned hot.

The sun had set and darkness grew, but he could see just fine in the dark. His eyes adjusted. Night birds chased each other between the trees, catching the occasional lingering white moth. A trio of foxes paused at the edge of the trees, watching him race through a clearing.

At the lake he stopped and drank a couple of handfuls of water from one of the streams that fed the lake. It was crisp and fresh. Sizzling in his mouth.

He turned down another path, a deer path and ran when he could. Walked when the branches were too many and too low, keeping his fire under control. Careful not to burn the forest.

This was the way that he, Skye, Pearce, Glenna and Adaire had walked through Faerie when they first returned from the human world. Pursued by Fomorians. He was sure of the direction. It had been a hot spring day. And the Luminary, Varion, had kept it summer all the time then. Roses in bloom. Luscious, ripe berries filled the vines. Greenery everywhere.

Unlike now. The Council had let Faerie run her natural course through the seasons, as she was meant to do, in Egan's opinion.

The trees stood mostly bare, the meadow plants having grown tall all summer, now turned yellow and dry. Not yet blasted by winter. But the natural world was shutting down. Gathering its energy and taking it deep down inside the earth. Preparing for another winter.

Egan walked and ran till dawn. He passed no villages. Just a web of deer trails. Eventually he passed one of the main roads. But that only confused him.

When they'd first returned to Faerie, they hadn't crossed any main roads. Not until after they reached the lake. And no one had been building new roads since then.

Egan finally had to admit it, he was lost.

He found a hollow at the foot of a mountain. It was all stone. He pulled a pile of dead brush into the clearing. Then found a downed tree and used his finger to shoot out a thin line of red hot flames. Just enough to burn a line through the trunk to cut it into pieces, like a laser. Not enough to set the whole thing on fire. Yet.

He carried the chunk of wood and set it on top of the pile of brush. Then repeated it until the tree trunk was mostly cut up.

Egan lit the whole pile on fire and undressed, leaving his clothes and boots on the nearby rocks. Then crawled inside the fire.

It wasn't the hottest fire he'd ever made and it wouldn't last long, but it would last a while. He fell asleep just as the sun came up.

CHAPTER 9 - SPIKE

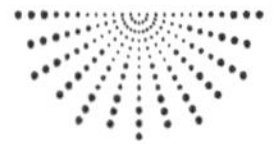

Spike left the caves just as the sky blazed orange and
pink with dawn. He shot off the edge, flapping his powerful
wings and catching an updraft. Once he'd risen above the tree
line, he flew towards the palace.

The air smelled fresh after yesterday's rain. The sky was clear
today and he could feel the air growing colder. Spike could see
almost forever. To the edges of Faerie. The tops of the forests still
had some red, orange and yellow leaves, mixed with green
needles of pines and yews. It was beautiful and just gazing at the
trees gave him a lift.

Spike dove down through a grassy area, scattering a drove of
hares he hadn't seen. The grayish tan creatures bounded for the
cover of bushes and rocks.

He climbed in height again, flapping his wings, feeling the
cool air whip past.

Would Dylan be at the palace? Or was he down at the lake,
still teaching young ones?

Spike's chest ached. He missed the Fae. He'd never known
Fae before, and felt a closeness to Dylan. Then the sprite had
been called to teach, to be an elder, and Spike hadn't seen him
since. That had been in the summer. When the dragons were

moving from their weirs outside of Faerie, back to the caves their ancestors had lived in. Within the boundaries of Faerie.

Now the dragons were tunneling ever deeper. Enlarging the caves and making new rooms. Creating for a home they could never be driven out of.

Spike saw the palace, high on its hill rising above the tree line in front of him. The massive trees which formed the pillars of the palace glistened in the morning sun.

He slowed down and could hear ravens screeching below him. Giving alarm. Spike glided in a wide circle over the buildings and plazas that formed the heart of Faerie. Giving time for any Fae to clear out of the courtyard. He slowed even more and simply dropped out of the sky onto the courtyard, only having to take one step to stop. Something the larger dragons would never perfect.

At the sound of his thunderous wings, several Fae came out of the palace to see who had arrived.

Once he'd stopped, Meredith and Solange came over to meet him. The other Fae just stood and watched. He knew dragons were still uncommon at the palace and that sometimes they brought news; news that was unwelcome.

"Hello Spike," said Meredith, putting a hand on his right elbow. "What brings you here this fine morning?"

Solange also put her hands on him. Stroking his dull scales. Which felt rather nice he had to admit.

"I bring a message to you from the wise ones. We do not know how to proceed with the Fomorians. We know the war continues, but we have tried all of our magic and nothing works. So we will remain in our caves and wait for your instructions."

Meredith bowed at him, "Thank you Spike. Please tell the wise ones that we continue to search for an answer as to the way to defeat the Fomorians. I appreciate their message and we will call on them when we have a plan."

Spike bowed at her in acknowledgement.

"How are the hatchlings?" asked Solange.

"They are troublesome. Unruly. But that is what hatchlings do best," he laughed with a hoarse croaking sound.

"Dylan will be here momentarily," said Meredith. "He was upstairs painting, but I called him."

Spike bobbed his head. It was the closest thing he could do to approximate that Fae gesture.

There were less Fae around than when Spike had normally come. He didn't know if there were others in the palace or if they were simply spread out throughout Faerie. Waiting for a plan, just like the dragons.

It seemed to take forever until Dylan arrived. He was naked except for green paint on his fingers. He seemed distracted, a faraway look on his face.

Meredith and Solange patted Spike, and walked back into the palace.

"Hello Spike, my friend."

"Dylan. It is good to see you."

"I must apologize for not coming to see you. I have no excuse. The world is wearing on me."

"How does the world 'wear on you'?"

"I don't know if dragons get depressed, but it feels awful. I'm always tired. And sad. about everything. Nothing seems worth the effort."

"What causes such a thing?" asked Spike.

"I don't know. But the presence of the Fomorians threatening us doesn't help."

"If I could remove them from the world, I would do it in an instant," said Spike.

"I know you would, my friend. I know you would. But until then, we must just keep going."

"Is there anything that will help?"

Dylan looked thoughtfully at him. "I don't know. I'm trying to paint. Solange told me to stop teaching. That wasn't helping me. I told Meredith that I'm done. She's not happy about it, but she accepted it. She found the water Fae a new teacher. One who doesn't know as much as I do, but the sprite will be happy to spend the winter at the bottom of the lake, teaching Fae and telling stories and sleeping. I just don't want to do that anymore. I want to be here in the palace with Solange."

"Good. That is good I think. To know what one wants."

"And how have you been?"

Spike told him about the chaos the hatchlings created and about being able to be in the circle with the wise ones last night. He didn't mention the fuchsia dragon.

"So does that mean you'll be allowed to sit with them every night?"

"I do not know," Spike said. "I have never seen them bring someone so young into their circle. But then most young dragons are too busy to sit and listen. I have sat and listened to them for years."

"I never did what most young Fae did either. I never fit in. I suppose that's why I was so eager to leave Faerie when it was closed. Not only did I not agree with the plan, but I wanted to see for myself what the human world was really like."

"And what was it like?" asked Spike. He'd only seen humans from a distance. Solange was the only human he'd ever actually met.

"Quite extraordinary actually. Humans are creative and dynamic. They're inventive. They have a drive to grow that's astonishing. They can also be mean, cruel and petty. Power hungry and selfish. Like Fae, and dragons, each one is an individual. I quite enjoyed living in their world. Despite having to spend my time wrapped in a human body."

"Is it better than living here? In this beautiful palace? With Solange near? And with other Fae from who you don't have to hide who you are?"

"No. But in the human world, the threat of war, of all Fae being extinguished wasn't there. At least I wasn't aware of it. The threat of your entire race being wiped out is disheartening."

"I can understand that," said Spike. "When we dragons lived

in the human world, even though we were invisible and we hoped humans wouldn't discover our existence, we were always afraid. That they'd stumble on our weirs, catch our shadows. Because we knew they would have used their machines to kill all of us."

"That must have been stressful for all of you," said Dylan.

"Yes. It is clear we feel safer now. This is the first batch of hatchlings we've had since we were banished from Faerie."

Dylan's mouth dropped open. And then he closed it.

"I, we, had no idea."

"We were always too afraid to increase our population. To have young. Our young are not careful. They are wild and reckless. And we try to watch them, but they do escape. It would have been a disaster for a young dragon to escape and be caught by humans because it couldn't hide itself yet. Or do other magic to protect itself. We couldn't take the risk."

At that moment there was a commotion on the plaza below the palace. Spike and Dylan walked to the edge.

There Spike saw something he hadn't seen since he had just learned to fly. A four-legged wyvern. So black it shone blue in the sunlight. Sleek and shiny, the young dragon, carried a sleeping Fae on its back. It climbed the steps up towards them, surrounded by other Fae. Who looked terribly worried.

Meredith and several others came running out of the palace, having been called, Spike guessed.

The young wyvern stared up at Spike with an amazed look.

"This creature is injured. I found it. It was trying to get to the palace. Is this the palace?"

"Yes this is the palace," said Spike. He had to look down at the wyvern who only came up to his elbow.

"Can I trust the creature to these others? They are not its kind. They don't have wings."

Aura walked up.

"I am her kind. You have done well, my friend, bringing her to us. Do you know what happened to her?"

"It was flying, but got tired. Then it walked. And talked with me. Telling me it would find someone to help me back home. I do not know what home is. Then it fell and I caught it before it hit the long stretch of flat rocks. I put it on my back and kept walking here.

"We will take care of her," said Aura. "May we lift her off your back?"

"Yes," said the wyvern, still suspicious.

"It is all right," said Spike. "You can trust these Fae."

Two earth spirits lifted the sylph from the wyvern's back. She was limp. And looked a pinkish color. Spike had seen this sylph before and knew she had light blue skin. A pink tone couldn't be a good thing. Unless sylphs could change color. Which perhaps they could. Fae were so complicated.

Dylan said, "I must follow them. Skye is my friend. I will call you. Perhaps you can take me to see the hatchlings."

"I would be honored too," said Spike.

Dylan followed the others into the palace.

Leaving Spike standing there with the young wyvern.

CHAPTER 10 - SOLANGE

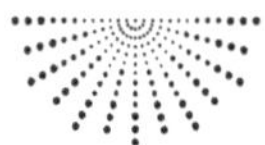

SOLANGE FOLLOWED AURA AND THE HEALERS, WILLOW AND Rush, as they took Skye up to a room on the second level of the palace. The palace simply created a room. It was light blue and airy looking. With gauzy, white curtains to filter the sun streaming in through huge, clear glass windows.

The room smelled strongly of oregano and sage. Solange finally spotted a dark blue bowl sitting on a table by the window. It held cut bundles of the herb, stems standing upright in water.

They lay Skye on a narrow, but tall bed. On her side, taking care to smoothly fold her thin wings in, so she wasn't lying on them.

"She is too hot," said Aura to Meredith.

Solange watched as Willow and Rush looked at Skye, then closed their eyes as they touched her. Solange knew they were doing things energetically that she didn't understand. Skye would have though. She was a wonderful healer.

Skye would be able to feel the energy flowing through the room as well. Solange knew it was there. Skye had talked to her about what Fae healers did. Solange could feel none of it.

She stood behind Aura and Meredith, wishing desperately for a cup of hot black tea. She hadn't gotten breakfast yet, had just been sitting down to eat when Spike arrived. She was thirsty and her stomach was growling, but she couldn't leave. Skye had become a good friend to her. Something told her that Skye needed her. The sylph's breath was raspy. Like she was wheezing. There was stuff in her lungs.

Solange had a room mate in college who had asthma. It had been under control, but when the poor girl caught pneumonia, added on top of a boatload of stress, her room mate had refused to get help until she was really, really sick. She too, had a lot of mucus in her lungs. She had sounded just like Skye, but Skye was Fae. Who knew what diseases they could get?

Finally, Willow said, "We do not know what is wrong with her. She is too hot, as you say. She feels depleted, and she is breathing badly. But it is more than that. There is a darkness inside her unlike anything we've ever seen."

"What should we do?" asked Meredith.

"Keep her cool is all we can think of at the moment," said the taller one, Rush. "With damp towels, particularly on her head and feet.

"Once she wakes, we can give her herbs with cooled medicinal tea," said Willow.

"We will return in a short time with some tea," said Rush.

They left the room.

Aura sank down on a stool next to the bed. Her face anguished.

Solange went to a water basin and soaked a nearby towel in it, wrung it out and put it on Skye's head. She repeated her actions with a second towel on the sylph's bare feet. Then got a third towel wet and put if on her naked torso.

She could hear Skye wheezing, as if there was liquid in her lungs.

Meredith asked, "Where was Skye yesterday?"

Aura said, "I sent her to the north. Where Fiachna and Egan reported seeing the offspring."

"And you heard nothing from her since?"

"No. She did not return, until now. I was about to send others out to look for her."

Meredith sat in a chair and threw her hands up in the air.

"What could have caused this?" she asked no one in particular.

Solange sat down across from Meredith.

"This is bad. She's having trouble breathing. If your healers can't heal her, she should be taken to a hospital. Neither of you should be in here with her. This might be contagious. If she got this sick so quickly. … "

Meredith looked at her, alarm crossing her face.

"You know we cannot take her to a hospital, and what do you mean, neither of us should be here? Are you immune to whatever this is?"

"We don't know what this is, but I'm not an elder either."

"Solange, you are not dispensable," said Meredith.

"No, I'm not, but I want both of you to leave now and go wash up with soap and water. Thoroughly. And tell the healers to do the same. No one comes in here without a mask over their face. I know Faerie doesn't have gloves and masks, but make some for the healers. I'll stay with Skye."

Meredith sighed deeply, "You're right, of course. Aura, come on, we're leaving."

Aura looked up, her face confused. It was clear she'd heard none of the conversation.

"Come dear," said Meredith, taking Aura's arm and helping the sylph elder to her feet. "We've got research to do."

Solange knew Meredith would take care of things, make sure everyone got as clean as possible. She'd spent enough time in the human world to gain an understanding of modern medicine and diseases.

She rewet the towel on Skye's forehead. Should she open the window?

The palace responded by opening the window itself.

"Thank you," said Solange, surprised.

Even though she knew nothing in Faerie should surprise her anymore. "If you've got any bright ideas about medication that would be lovely."

There was no response.

Solange kept wetting towels. When Willow brought up tea, Solange took it from her, but wouldn't let her in the door. Which made the healer really angry.

"Please go speak with Meredith. It's really important. She'll explain."

Willow left.

Once Skye woke up. Solange helped her sit up and sip some of the cold tea.

"How do you feel?"

"Wretched." Skye coughed.

"Here, here's a bowl. Spit that crap out."

Skye did. It looked slimy, green and awful.

"You need antibiotics," said Solange.

"No. Fae can't have them."

"Well, what would help?"

Skye shrugged.

"Rest. I'm cold." Skye was shivering.

Solange touched the sylph's forehead, which felt cool.

"You lie down. On your other side. I'll cover you up."

Skye did as she was told and Solange collected the wet towels and put them in the basin of water. A blue down comforter lay draped over a wooden rack near the bed.

"Please close the window," she asked the palace.

And it did.

She spread the comforter over Skye, taking care not to bend her folded wings. The sylph stopped shivering soon after and drifted back to sleep.

Solange sat and listened to her rasping breathing.

She needed soap and water too. And a clean towel. As soon as she thought it, the palace provided it. An actual sink with running water appeared on one wall. Plumbing existed on the ground floor, but hadn't up on this level before.

Solange scrubbed her hands and forearms with lavender soap until the skin felt raw. But clean. Then she dried thoroughly with the clean towel.

The room was quite chilly. Daylight gone and it would be a cold fall night. Perhaps even frosty. The palace built a small fire and Solange tossed everything in the bowl into it. Burn up those germs, even if it meant burning the towels. Then she rinsed out the bowl under hot running water. Then covered her hands with soap again, squeezing the foam into the bowl and rinsing it again and again. Leaving it to dry by the fire.

She washed her hands again, wrapped herself in a blanket and sat by the fire in the darkness. More for comfort than cold.

And hoped that whatever Skye had, wouldn't travel to anyone else. Especially her.

CHAPTER 11 - LEA

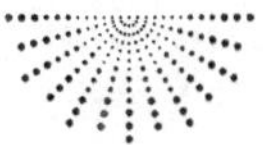

LEA STOOD IN THE BURNT OUT CLEARING, LOOKING AT HER charges. It was getting colder and colder these mornings. There had been a frost last night, although not a hard, killing frost.

Brian and Ogden had decided she should take charge of this meadow. Neither one of them knew it well enough, but she had. She would help the forest decay faster and begin planting those smaller things which had once thrived here, when there had more sun that reached the soil. The land might have done that anyway. Fae simply helped speed up the process and in this case, plant things which were becoming more rare. Returning balance to the land.

In front of her stood two older dryads. And another so young she barely knew all the plant names. And then there were the dragons. A huge silver sparkly thing who looked wrinkled and elderly. And a younger black dragon with ruffles around his neck.

The two dragons made her want to shake with fear.

She picked up a piece of dried moss instead and nervously began teasing it apart.

The wind changed direction and brought the scent of the charred wood to her. She wrinkled her nose at the smell.

"The first thing we will do here is remove most of the dead trees that are standing. And the newly downed logs. We can leave a couple of the older rotting logs. They will provide nice soil someday. We need to remove things with a minimum of trampling down the soil. Is that possible?"

She looked at the dragons.

The black one said, "If you humans can cut the standing trees off, then I can fly in and lift them out. Or would you prefer I pull them out roots and all? I can lift the logs that are lying down by flying in although I might have to land first. Those will be heavier, filled with water from the rain."

"I think it would be better to cut the still standing trees. Pulling out the roots will disturb everything. Their roots are all connected like a giant underground web. It covers this entire area."

The dragon bobbed his head in acknowledgement.

She assigned the older dryads, Ash with the smooth, grayish skin, and Holly with the furrowed skin which reminded her of holly bark, to cut down the trees, showing them the two that should remain standing. The black dragon, Ruffles, took to the air, hovering above the clearing. The dryads went to work cutting a tree and before it even fell Ruffles had grabbed it and lifted it away from them, ferrying it out of the area.

Lea turned to the other two. The young Fae with very short, green and glossy, curly hair, whose name was Thyme, and the silver dragon.

"What can the two of you do to help?"

"I am strong," said the young Fae. "I can help gather roots and plant them."

"I am not strong enough to help Ruffles," said the silver dragon, whose name it turned out was Silver. "But once you tell me something, I will never forget it. And I came primarily to watch, but if there is something I can do, I will be pleased to help. I can dig deep with my claws, although I do have big feet and I'd be afraid I might step on something precious."

"Good, so you know your own drawbacks. That's a wise thing."

"Well, I am nearly as old as these hills," said Silver. "It would be a pity if I had not gained any wisdom in my long life."

Lea laughed. She'd had no idea dragons came with a sense of humor.

While Ash, Holly and Ruffles cleared the land, Lea took Thyme along a path to another meadow. Silver flew above them since the path was quite narrow.

Lea had digging tools, large woven bags and a willow basket to carry roots in.

This meadow was mostly humousy, lime soil, although there were a few large limestone boulders in it.

The dragon landed on one of them.

Lea directed Thyme to a patch of comfrey. The leaves were brown and withered. The young one could begin with these nearly indestructible roots.

"They go very deep, nearly to the other side of the earth, but you do not need all of the root. Just a piece as long as your forearm will be fine."

Thyme set to work, digging the roots and putting them in a bag.

Lea went over to the dragon.

"You see these here, these are stone crop," she said, pointing to the grayish white succulents lining the crevice on the side of the boulder the dragon sat on. "It will take gentle, fine work. You'll need to pry them out, roots and all if you can, without breaking too much of the top off. Then set them gently in the bottom of this basket. Half of these will be enough."

"Oh, I think I can do that," said Silver.

Lea moved off to another part of the meadow, digging up roots of fringe cups, three cornered garlic, toadflax, meadow foam, toothwort and many others. She soon had all three bags filled. But couldn't carry them far all at once.

Thyme finished with the comfrey and helped carry the bags over to Silver.

She'd done a delicate job digging out the stonecrop.

Silver volunteered to fly the heavy bags back to the other meadow. She grabbed them with her clawed feet and lifted off. Thyme carried the basket and Lea the digging tools.

By the time they got to the other meadow, Silver was already there, having landed with the bags of roots.

All but three of the downed logs were gone, and all but two of the dead trees cleared. Ruffles was using his tail to sweep off a large flat boulder, clearing it of most of the decayed log debris.

There was another larger boulder on the other side of the new meadow. Silver landed on that one and swept it clean with her tail.

Ash and Holly were breaking apart the downed logs, opening up to the rotted centers, which would make perfect soil for some of the plants.

Lea's heart leapt at so much done quickly and well. The entire area was ready to plant.

She motioned for Ash, Holly and Thyme to pick a bag and begin planting.

"Plant in clusters, the same plants together. That is best to begin with."

She took the basket and divided half the stone crop for Silver and the other half for Ruffles. She showed him how to put some soil in a crevice and then the plants root first.

Then she took a bag and began planting.

By the time the sun had passed below the tree line, they had finished.

"This will be beautiful," said Ash.

"I certainly hope so. We still have more plants to add. But I think that will wait until spring. We can collect seedlings to plant then," said Lea.

"What do we do next," asked Silver.

"Next, we'll work on another area. A woodland, also badly damaged. What did you do with the logs?" Lea asked Ruffles.

"I took them to our caves. We always need wood for fires. Shall we meet again tomorrow?" asked Ruffles.

"Yes, tomorrow. The time for planting will soon run out. Once the freezes start we are done until spring, other than cleaning up."

"Where shall we meet?" asked Silver.

"Let us we meet at the other meadow? It is closer to the woodland that needs help."

"This is so much fun," said the older dragon.

Lea looked at her in surprise.

"Well, is it not?" asked Silver.

"Yes, it is, but then I am an earth spirit. It never occurred to me that dragons would consider this fun."

"It is a game. We plant these tiny plants or roots and then when their time is right, they grow, and we will all be surprised at what it looks like."

"You are right. It is just like that," said Lea, smiling.

She watched the dragons fly off and the dryads skipping along in front of her as they returned to the nearest village. Lea followed them at a much slower pace, returning the tools, bags and basket to a common storage shed.

She wasn't hungry, so she returned to the forest and found a lovely mossy hollow to curl up in for the evening. She lay there basking in the sounds of the forest and considering what life as a dragon must be like.

CHAPTER 12 - SKYE

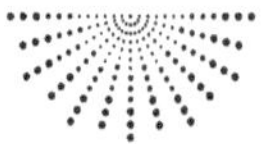

Skye woke in the middle of the night. She felt hot and there was a down comforter covering her. She didn't move, not even to open her eyes.

Where was she?

The last thing she remembered was being on the road, with the young dragon. But now she was inside somewhere. It was dark, she could tell that even with her eyes closed.

She could smell herbs. Sage and something else. And someone or something was nearby. She could hear them breathing softly, when she held her own breath. Which was loud and filled with fluid. Her lungs were a mess.

Finally, she could stand the heat no more. She opened her eyes and saw a high ceilinged room. With large windows through which the moon shone in, lighting the room slightly. She hurled the comforter off and sat up.

There was a dark shape lying down on a couch near the fire. Huddled in another comforter and obviously asleep. She recognized the energy of the person on the couch. Not Fae, human. Solange.

Without the comforter Skye felt cool enough. Everything around her told her she was in Faerie, in the palace. Safe.

Skye tried to understand what was happening. Her lungs were the problem. No, the symptom, she had an infection. Where had she gotten something so strong?

Then she saw a shape. The black Fomorian. Plague, Fiachna had name him. He'd been there watching the earthquake and the trees blow down. Skye had an image of him spitting at the wind and it carrying his spittle to her. He was the problem.

"Plague," she said, loudly. Her throat and mouth dry, so it came out like a croaking sound.

There was a rustling noise on the couch and Solange was up and on her feet.

"What?"

"Plague," Skye said again.

"I'll get you a glass of water."

Skye heard glass clinking against metal and water running. Then Solange was there with a glass. Skye held in it her shaking hands and sipped. The cool water flowed down her throat, loosening up more mucous. Then Skye handed the glass back, noticing Solange didn't touch it in the same place she had.

"Plague. Tell Meredith or Aura, Plague. He got to me through the boundary. Stay safe."

She felt so weak now. She coughed and Solange held out a bowl.

"Spit," Solange demanded.

Skye spit out some gross crap and lay back down.

"Are you cold?" she heard Solange say.

"Not yet."

Then she was gone. Lost in nightmares about the Fomorians. That they could reach through the boundary of Faerie and infect them all.

CHAPTER 13 - FIACHNA

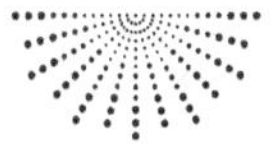

FIACHNA AND THE OTHERS LEFT THE BARROW AFTER THE storm passed. They sky was clear and bright with the half moon.

They crested the hill and he saw the Fomorians huddled around a fire just past the boundary of Faerie. Immediately he and the other stone Fae melded into the rocks.

The Fomorians were taking apart an old wooden building and burning it. It wasn't big. Maybe it had been a shed of some sort. Twenty years ago. The fire was blazing high enough to keep the giants warm.

He smelled roasting meat. They'd caught something and were cooking it. A cow perhaps? Cows often grazed the area near Faerie, or maybe it was a sheep.

The meat smelled good and made his mouth water as Fiachna realized he'd missed a few meals. They all had. The air felt freezing. There would be frost again tonight.

It must be Samhain already. He never kept track of such things. It was winter when it felt like winter. And he'd rarely been around others for the last millennia. He'd always been out alone, walking the boundaries of Faerie, making sure they were secure. Just like tonight. Except he had company. He'd have preferred to be alone, if he couldn't be with Clare.

Two of the Fomorians were yelling at each other. Corb of the sea and Conand of the north wind. The two of them were shimmering in and out of their giant-like forms, and back to sea and wind. The argument turned into blows and the others formed a circle around them. Watching and encouraging the fight.

Conand blew Corb over, wind coming out his mouth. Corb shot a stream of water right back at Conand, knocked him down. They both scrambled up, in giant form. Their fists pummeled each other, amidst the occasional blast of wind or water.

They were the same size and equally as strong. The fight kept on for what seemed like hours with neither winning or losing. They were both bleeding from cuts by fists, or from landing on the stony ground.

Pearce moved up beside Fiachna. "Can we learn anything from this? They can't even win over each other."

Fiachna shook his head. He didn't know what they might learn from the fight.

Pearce said, "They'll fight all night. Sleep all day, stuffed with roasted meat. And then do it all over again. I wish they'd go to the other side of the world and do it."

"I keep thinking that if we watch them long enough, we will find a weakness. A way in to getting rid of them."

"I know. But it hasn't worked yet," said Pearce.

"No. No, it has not.

"So we need another tactic."

"Like what?" asked Fiachna, staring the younger stone Fae in the eyes.

"Faerie has been living in fear and stagnation ever since the Fomorians arrived. We've tried locking them up. Tried locking them out, hiding. They're still there, waiting. We've heard Balor say he just wants to destroy Faerie. What if we let him? Open the boundaries and give him the illusion that Faerie is being destroyed by them. Everything they touch withers. Might the Fomorians just give up and leave? Weren't they once a settled people who grew cattle and grain and farmed food? If we portray Faerie as a ruined place, then perhaps they'd just go find someplace greener and fertile and go back to who they were, their vengeance sated."

"It's a nice idea, but the place they'd probably take over would be the human world."

"I lived in the human world for over a thousand years," said Pearce. "I loved many humans, but does Faerie have to sacrifice itself for them?"

"I don't know," said Fiachna. He thought of Clare. He'd sacrifice himself for her without hesitation. But would he sacrifice all of Faerie for her?

Fiachna watched the fight, still going on, although the combatants were slower to get up after falling.

He said to Pearce, "It is time for someone to report back. You go and speak to the Council. See what they make of your idea. I am not sure it would work. I think the Fomorians would stay for a very long time to make sure we are all dead. We had a hard enough time maintaining the illusion of ruin in order to get them from the vault to outside the boundary. To maintain it for years upon years, I do not think it possible. And they will be looking for trickery from now on."

Pearce nodded. "It was just a thought, but I'll go report in and tell them. Then I'll return."

And with that he was gone.

His departure left Fiachna with ideas to chew on while he watched the two Fomorians fight each other to exhaustion.

CHAPTER 14 - EGAN

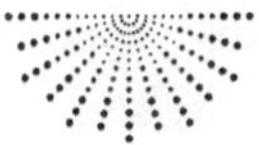

Egan woke lying in the cold ashes. His scales dulled by the ashes. He stood, his body aching from walking so much the day before. And the day before that. And the day before that.

He sipped a bit of water from a stream trying to clear his head. The water tasted dull, not refreshing like usual. At least it wasn't bitingly cold.

Even his head ached from sleeping stiff and cramped in a cold fire last night.

He sat down on a large stone, feeling the chill of it through his thick skin. He cradled his head in his hands, trying to massage the pain away.

If he could just find the point where he and the others had entered Faerie, then perhaps that would help him find Lassair's village.

He'd found three villages yesterday. None of them hers and no one had ever even heard of a fire Fae named Lassair who did pepper magic. One of the villages had consisted only of fire Fae. He could still smell the smoke from their fires. He'd longed to stay, but she hadn't been there. He should have at least spent the night in that village, but it had been so early in the day.

And he'd been afraid to stay.

Afraid that if he stayed, he'd take the easy way and never come back out of the fire.

He'd never in his life taken the easy way, but since returning to Faerie and the magical accident, he hadn't exactly been himself. He now knew what all the other elements felt like. He'd lived with them inside himself.

After all the other elements had been extracted, he still wasn't himself. He doubted himself constantly. Couldn't do things he used to be able to do effortlessly. He'd become weak and less than himself.

That's what came from slamming a door shut when it opened for you.

That door had been Lassair.

He rubbed his eyes and sat up straighter. He had probably wandered the length of Faerie, except in circle after circle. Had no one ever made a map of Faerie before?

He knew the answer to that before the idea popped into his head. Many people had. Each map more inaccurate than the last, because Faerie was continually changing. To suit herself.

So, if he wasn't finding Lassair, it was because Faerie didn't want him to or it wasn't the right time yet.

"So what is it that you *do* want me to do?" he asked, out loud. An image of the northwest section of Faerie popped into his mind. He suddenly knew *that* wasn't where Lassair's village was.

"Okay. What am I supposed to be looking for?"

Silence.

Egan got up and began walking. At least he knew where he was. So, he could get to where Faerie wanted him to go. He had no idea what he'd do when he got there.

CHAPTER 15 - SPIKE

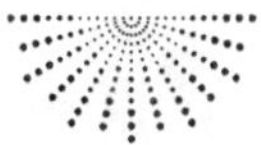

Spike stood in the empty courtyard in front of the palace with the wyvern. He wanted to give the wyvern time to adjust to him.

So he looked elsewhere.

Spike noticed that frost lay everywhere, most visible in the cracks between the perfectly square stones which made up the courtyard. Normally a golden color, this morning they glowed white like the night stars.

Winter was come.

A good time to be sitting in front of a warm fire with a nice full belly.

He had the full belly still, but no fire. He remembered the flavor of the roasted deer from yesterday quite clearly. The rich juices trapped inside the succulent meat even after it was flamed by a dragon's fire.

A whiff of smoke caught the wind and blew down towards them. It was coming out of the top of the palace. They had fires going.

All the Fae had gone into the palace, not that there had been many. He knew most of the water Fae had probably gone to the bottom of the lake. It was getting too cold out for fire Fae.

They'd gone into fires. The sylphs mostly thrived in the cold. Maybe they were out flying. Or in their own caverns where they lived. Earth spirits might be out in the woods. Or maybe they lived inside during winter.

He stopped puzzling about the whereabouts of all the Fae and turned to the larger mystery beside him.

"Why do you not know what home is?"

"If I knew what it was, perhaps I could find it," said the wyvern. Who, upon looking at the small dragon, seemed younger and younger.

"It's where you live. Where you were hatched."

"It was in a warm, dark place."

"A cave?" asked Spike.

"I do not know what a cave is."

"It's a hole in the earth. Sometimes in a mountain."

"It was deep in the earth. The ground was flat."

"When were you hatched?"

"The sun has come up five times since I broke out of my shell."

"And the other wyverns who cleaned and fed you?"

"I was the only one. There were four other eggs, but I grew tired of waiting for them."

Spike stared at the little one.

"There were no full grown wyverns there?"

"No."

"That is very curious," said Spike. "Are you hungry?"

"Yes. I ate the second sunrise after I was hatched. I caught a small animal and ate it, but I haven't eaten since then. When the, what did you call her, Fae? When she flew by, I tried to catch her thinking I would eat her, but then she spoke to me. I knew I could not eat anything that talked to me."

"Good. Fae are not for eating. Fly with me back to our weir. I shall introduce you to our wise ones and you can eat. Then we'll set about finding where you were hatched."

"Will they eat me?"

"No. Not if you talk to them," said Spike, wryly.

He ran off the edge of the courtyard, flapping his large wings to gain height. The wyvern followed him, but gained height much faster. He remembered that wyverns were very fast and sleek dragons.

The wyvern's flight was erratic, sprinting and slowing to catch its breath. Then sprinting again. The young one didn't have any endurance yet.

"Let me know if you want to land and rest," sent Spike. There was no answer. The wyvern probably didn't know how to send. Or perhaps it couldn't. Maybe wyverns were quite different than other dragons.

They flew on, finally Spike sighted the mountain that contained the dragon caves. He began to descend, the wyvern following.

By the time they dove for the wide cave mouth, it was crowded with dragons. Who moved aside to open a space for the two to land.

Spike landed only taking a couple of steps before stopping. Then moved out of the way.

The wyvern didn't slow quickly enough and tumbled to a stop, running into Ethelgarde.

"Yee yee yee," it shrieked.

Whether in surprise or pain, Spike wasn't sure. But he rushed over to the wyvern's side and helped right the young one.

They were surrounded by three circles of dragons. Countless heads peered at them. They were standing in the center.

"Are you okay?" Spike asked.

"Yes. I do not land well."

"You have time to learn. I did not land well when I was young either."

"Really?" asked the wyvern, looking up hopefully.

"Really. This is Ethelgarde."

Ethelgarde bowed and asked, "What is your name?"

"I do not have a name yet. It, she, the Fae, asked me the same thing. How do I catch a name?"

"You can choose one yourself or let others name you," said Ethelgarde.

"Him," said the wyvern, pointing to Spike. "He should name me."

Spike was silent and looked out at the sky, remembering the wyvern's speed. "I name you Bluefire after the fast stars that shoot across the sky."

"Thank you. That is a wonderful name. I shall try to be like that," said the wyvern.

"Come, let us get you some food," said Spike.

He led Bluefire over to one of the fire pits, tore off a hunk of meat from a carcass roasting in the flames and gave it to the wyvern who chewed on it delicately.

Ethelgarde asked, "Where did she come from?"

"She?" asked Spike.

"She. Black-blue wyverns are always she."

"One of the Fae flew past her and attracted Bluefire's attention. The Fae took her back to the palace. That's where I met her. She's only five days old and doesn't know where she was hatched. There are four other eggs, but apparently, no full grown wyverns."

Silver said, "Wyvern eggs do not always hatch when they are supposed to. Sometimes entire cycles of seasons pass before they break open. It is possible the adults are dead, I suppose. I have never heard of eggs taking that long. The wyverns had long disappeared when we left Faerie. I would think the Fae would know if any had stayed behind."

"One would think," said Attania, rustling her wings thoughtfully.

"After she finishes eating, bring her to us. We have many questions. Tomorrow we will go search for her weir, and see if we can find adults or bring back the other eggs to care for them," said Ethelgarde.

Spike caught a flash of fuchsia going back down the tunnel to where the hatchlings lived. He really would like to speak with that beautiful dragon someday. Find out her name. Fly somewhere together with her.

He turned and moved closer to the cook fire, waiting for the wyvern. Only taking one bite of meat himself, in order to quench his thirst. The juices of the meat ran down his throat, filled with the rich, fatty flavor of sheep.

So, someone had been hunting outside of Faerie.

Finally, Spike made the wyvern stop, before she ate herself senseless and wouldn't be able to answer any questions. He led her back to the grotto where the wise ones talked.

CHAPTER 16 - SOLANGE

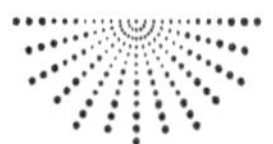

Solange had stayed with Skye for three days now. The sylph seemed to get neither better nor worse.

She was always in the throes of either a fever or chills. The windows wide open or shut with a blazing fire in the fireplace.

Mostly Skye slept. The few times she woke, Solange was able to get some broth or medicinal tea down her throat. And let Skye cough up some of the gross stuff that inhibited her breathing.

Solange's skin was raw from scrubbing herself clean. The healers left her a salve made from lavender, which Solange knew had antibacterial properties. She rubbed it on her hands, hoping it would heal the cracks which were forming from washing so often.

She didn't know if what Skye had was bacterial or viral. Did she have pneumonia or some form of plague, like she'd mentioned?

Solange couldn't remember much about the Black Death. Only that the disease vector had been fleas. But there were also plagues that looked like pneumonia.

In the end she had no information and could only hope that Skye's strong Fae body would heal itself, with pathetic little help from Solange.

Through the closed door, Solange gave Meredith the message about Plague reaching Skye through the boundary. Solange didn't know what it meant, not really. But Meredith sounded afraid.

Food and beverages were sent up, and left outside the door. Solange would let no one in the room. Not even the healers. Not even Dylan. Well, especially not Dylan. She explained to them about the plague. Faerie had no experience with plagues. The human world had plenty. It was bad enough she'd been exposed. Solange would allow no one else to be exposed. Luckily, they saw her point. Meredith had lived in the human world for millennia and Solange suspected the elder was helping keep others away.

Dylan came every morning and night, and stood outside the door talking to her.

She could tell he was depressed. He put a cheerful tone into his voice, which is how she knew. She kept telling him to go paint something new. He said he was. She didn't know whether to believe him or not.

Meredith assured her that no one else had gotten sick.

Solange washed their dirty dishes in the sink. And kept the spacious room as clean as possible without allowing anything to leave it.

The palace supplied fresh firewood everyday. And even some old manuscripts from the library for her to read while Skye slept. It didn't offer medicine. The palace also probably had no knowledge of plagues.

The manuscripts were about wyverns, of all things. She wasn't far into the stack before realizing it was a wyvern that brought Skye back. Solange had been around Faerie long enough to know that the palace always left books out in the library for a reason. If you found one open when you entered, the palace had decided it was the information you needed to have, and it was a good idea to read it.

Solange sipped a cup of black tea, hot only because she'd set the teapot near the fire, and spread out one of the fragile manuscripts on the large oak table. She pulled up a wooden chair and gently paged through it.

It showed paintings of various wyverns. Some red, some green, others bluish black. Most had only two legs, but there were two paintings of four-legged wyverns.

The text said that the four-legged ones were extremely rare and quite lethal. They had a particularly venomous bite. Unlike other dragons, wyverns rarely breathed fire.

They had been seldom seen even in Faerie, even in the distant past. They hadn't lived with the other dragons, preferring to be solitary.

Solange fell asleep reading the text and woke up long enough to rise and go lie down on the couch. Covering herself with the comforter, even though it was the middle of the day.

She dreamt about wyverns. The bluish black one. And four others who were green and crimson. All the others only had two legs. They were fast and flew with darting motions.

They were hunting. Attacking someone, chasing them over a green and rocky field. It looked human, no lumpier. Was it a water Fae? It was liquid looking. But different from Meredith or Dylan. And larger, almost as tall as the wyverns. It was nighttime and difficult for her to see. They were biting, flashing in to attack. Retreating when it fought back at them. They punctured it enough and their prey began to bleed.

Then one of the wyverns, a red one, turned on her.

Solange screamed herself awake to find herself on the couch, shaking. Covered with the comforter and sweating. She pulled it off and stood up, trying to wake up.

And began coughing.

CHAPTER 17 - LEA

Lea stood in the meadow, waiting for the others to arrive. It was Samhain. The first day of winter, and the weather was showing it.

Snowflakes drifted down catching on her hair, lashes and the thin brown jacket she wore over a cotton tunic and pants. She'd even worn leather boots and work gloves.

The air smelled crisp and full of potential. Everything felt peaceful. Although she knew that wasn't true. The war, the standoff, was still going on. But she had work to do. Because war, or no, life went on.

The dragons arrived first. The breath coming out of their snouts formed smokey spirals in the cold air. The ground wasn't frozen solid yet, especially under the tree cover, but she'd been right yesterday. This would be the last day they could plant.

"Good morning," Lea said.

"Good morning," said Silver. "And what a glorious morning."

"Hello," said Ruffles, rubbing his eyes.

"You like snow?" Lea asked Silver.

"I love snow. There's nothing like looking down at the entire world covered with snow. It's so beautiful."

"I would imagine it is," said Lea. She'd never considered what flying over snow would look like.

Eventually, Thyme arrived. Wearing a jacket, pants, boots and gloves, just like Lea. Her clothes were all in red, except the brown leather boots.

"I do not think Holly and Ash are coming," she said. "They did not come to meet me. I waited for a long time."

"Well, more's the pity," said Lea. "It is a beautiful day to be out in the woods. Let us move on to the woodland, shall we? It's just over this hill. I believe the path is wide enough for the two of you to walk it. One behind the other," she motioned towards the dragons.

Lea led the way through the meadow they'd dug in yesterday. She carried bags filled with bulbs and roots, which had been gathered days before. The bags weren't as heavy as yesterday's. Bulbs didn't weigh as much as damp, muddy roots.

The meadow was now a white lumpy landscape with the occasional large stone poking up. A few shrubs still held their shape, branches outlined with snow.

The entire meadow shone with a million white and rainbow crystals as the sun came out from behind the clouds.

"Oh," said Silver, behind her, holding her breath.

Lea stopped and admired the beauty around her.

Then they continued on. The snow wasn't deep, even out in the meadow. Just the width of a finger, maybe two. Enough to make things look lovely and to make the announcement that winter was here.

Once beneath the yews, there was little snow. Only in places where damaged trees had been taken out.

The yews were old and massive. Lea couldn't even put her arms around their trunks. In taking out the trees damaged by the war, the ground had been trampled. Or perhaps that had happened during the battle, she wasn't sure.

She set the four bags down gently.

"I have five different types of plants here. There is so much dry shade here, it is difficult to grow things, but we will try. I have the roots of dog tooth violets and primroses. And bulbs of snowdrops, cyclamen and lily of the valley. None of them are planted very deeply, but it would be helpful to dig down deeply to loosen up the soil, unless there are a lot of tree roots in the area. We do not want to disturb the trees more than they already have been. Perhaps if we paired up; Thyme with Ruffles and I will work with Silver. The dragons can dig with their claws, and we Fae can plant. Clump like things together and then a bit farther away, a clump of something else."

Thyme nodded.

"This is going to be fun," said Silver.

"Oh, and start at the far side and let us work our way back here, so we do not walk on where we planted. You two take that half and we will take this half.

Silver moved to the far end of the woodland as Lea picked out a bunch of snowdrop bulbs, putting them in one pocket. Then put cyclamen in another pocket. She carried some primula roots in her gloved hands.

They worked quickly at first, slowing down as they became colder.

Silver asked questions about the plants. What did each one look like? Did they have medicinal properties or were they simply pretty? When would they bloom? Spring? Summer? Fall?

The dragon had a zest for life and a desire to learn which surprised Lea.

"Where do you live?" asked Silver.

"I used to live near the center of Faerie. Then during the war things became chaotic. I went into the forest to live. I was captured by some of the Fomorians. Their offspring, rather. They put a spell on me and changed me into a fox. I lived as a fox for many seasons. Since I have been returned to Fae form, I have lived in the forest, always moving. Alone. Sometimes going into villages for a time. It is a difficult life for one as old as I am, but I have not found a place I feel at home. Or safe," said Lea.

"That is a sad story. It is difficult to thrive when one feels always afraid. When we dragons were cast out of Faerie, into the human world, I felt fear. All the time. We were invisible, but always at risk of being discovered by humans. Who would have exterminated us all. There was such relief when we were allowed to return to Faerie again. Now we have hatchlings for the first time since before we left."

"For the first time? You mean there have been no baby dragons in the entire time you were gone?"

"We were too afraid," said Silver. She paused and then continued, "I was too young to lay eggs when I lived here before. And now I am far too old. I will never have young of my own."

"I am sorry," said Lea. "I will never have a child either. The forest is my child."

"That is a good child to have. I will help raise the hatchlings that we have. Teach them if they want to learn."

They continued working, magic flowing through their fingers until all the bulbs and roots were planted. She'd planned right, they had had enough to cover the entire section of the forest.

By the time they finished, Lea felt cold and sore from the work. Her back ached and her fingers were numb. Thyme said she was cold. The child was far too young to be achy.

Silver and Ruffles flew off with promises to help again in the spring.

Lea walked Thyme back to her village. She returned the tools and the bags.

Then stood by a cook fire in the center of the village warming herself. And watching the snow fall. Trying to decide where to spend the night.

CHAPTER 18 - SKYE

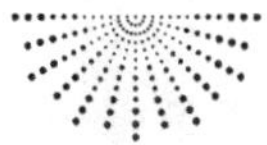

IT WAS DARK WHEN SKYE WOKE. SHE FELT WRETCHED, BUT knew her breathing was better. Her head felt like an elephant had stomped on it, and her entire body ached. She felt weak. Plus, she stank and was sweaty. The window was closed and it was too hot. She tossed the comforter off once again and sat up.

Her head throbbed, but she could think clearly. At least she felt more clear that she had in days. There was a fire blazing in the fireplace. Solange lay on the couch, covered with a comforter and shivering.

Skye stood and drank some water from a glass on the table. It tasted so clean and sweet. She vaguely remembered Solange helping her drink some vile tasting medicinal tea the healers had made.

As she stood watching Solange, Skye slowly realized that whatever Plague had given her, she'd passed on to Solange. And the human was really sick.

She should get her onto the bed.

"Palace, can I have some dim light please?"

Two oil lamps were immediately lit.

"And clean linens for the bed?"

A thwap, thwap sound came from the bed and Skye walked over to find the palace had just put clean sheets on it. Amazing.

Skye went over to Solange, pulled the comforter off and lifted her, carrying the human over to the bed. She lay her down and slipped off the woman's leather shoes. Her clothes were drenched, so Skye pulled them off and tossed them into the corner.

The comforter had been damp too, but there was a clean, folded one on a ledge by the window. Skye got it and spread it over Solange, tucking her in. She arranged the pillows so that Solange was a bit more upright and could breathe better. The wheezing was worrisome.

"I don't suppose you have any medicine for this nasty disease, do you palace?"

Nothing happened. Skye hadn't thought it would. She would have to take care of it, but she needed to rest a bit first.

Skye sat in the chair at the table. There was an untouched bowl of cold soup there. A clean spoon lay next to the bowl. Skye ate a few spoonfuls. It was rich and satisfying. There was chicken in it, carrots and leeks. Before she knew it, the bowl was empty.

Skye planted her feet solidly on the wood floor. And felt just how low her energy level was. She pulled some power up from the earth below, up through the palace, up through the soles of her feet. Felt it travel up her legs to her center. She drew energy down from above, from the sky, the stars and the moon. Down through her head, her neck, her chest. Felt the two energies meeting in her center, combining and melding together.

Then she went over to the bed. Skye held her hands over Solange, beginning at her head and moving down to her toes.

She could feel the infection. It was everywhere. The worst part was in her lungs, choking her air supply, which pumped her heart, and fed her blood. Everything was shutting down.

Skye went to work on Solange's lungs. Adding heat, helping to dry up the mucus collecting there. Helping her to breathe deeper, so her heart would work better. Helping Solange fight the infection. Skye worked on her for as long as she could.

Then Skye felt Solange's forehead. The woman had cooled down a bit.

Skye tossed a couple of pieces of firewood on the fire and lay down on the couch with the comforter she'd used on the bed.

She slept till dawn.

CHAPTER 19 - FIACHNA

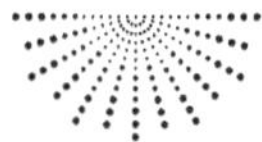

FIACHNA LED THE STONE WARRIORS NORTHWARD, JUST INSIDE the western boundary of Faerie. They followed the Fomorians who seemed to be tracking something. Elatha was often stopping to look at the ground.

It was easier to stay hidden here. The land was forested with much undergrowth. Even though the trees and bushes had lost their leaves, much of the forest here was evergreen. The yews and pines cast a dense shade. In the sunny spots strawberry trees and junipers grew.

Amongst it all stood thickets of twiggy branches to hide behind, so the Fae could save their energy, their magic for when they needed it most. It was slow going, especially through the thorny wild rose thickets.

The Fomorians didn't seem to be in a great hurry.

The farther north they went, took them away from the sea. Patches of snow began to cover the land. Not beneath the trees of Faerie, but out in the open meadows. The Fomorians were easy to spot against the white snow. They weren't making any effort to hide.

Why should they?

As far as Fiachna could tell they were invincible. If they had weaknesses other than arrogance, lack of discipline and stupidity, he had yet to see them. As far as he could tell, none of their weaknesses were fatal. At least to them.

He was hoping that Balor's thirst for vengeance would kill the giant. Fiachna searched for a way to use that against them, but had found nothing, so far.

The Fomorians stopped. They'd found what looked like the remains of a large fire. Balor motioned to Conand and Dela. The two of them went to the other side of the meadow and Conand blew down a couple of shrubby looking trees. The two of them dragged the wood back to the fire and piled it up.

Balor removed all his head coverings with one swipe. He had his back to Fiachna, who knew the giant was looking at the firewood with the baleful eye in the middle of his forehead. The wood caught fire and began to burn quickly.

Amazing, considering it was probably green, wet wood. Balor put the cloths back on his head, covering the eye. By then, Conand and Dela had brought back more wood for the fire.

The sun was beginning to set beneath the tall yews. It was cold. He could feel it through his boots, but stone Fae were used to cold. That wasn't what bothered him.

He was weary of always being on the move, and at least for the present, not being particularly useful.

He motioned for Alain to take the first watch. The Fae nodded and sidled up into the shadow of a gnarled yew.

Fiachna sat down, leaning his back against a large chunk of limestone. He closed his eyes to sleep, but it didn't come.

He felt a deep rumbling in the earth. It was coming from one of the mountains inside Faerie. Was it mountain where the dragons' caves were? Few stone Fae would be able to hear the sound unless they were listening for it. It was a subtle vibration far, far beneath the earth. Why were the dragons digging so deep? Surely, they hadn't had that many eggs?

Perhaps they knew something he didn't. Fiachna searched

the surrounding stones and those farther away, looking for answers. To any question.

How could the Fae rid themselves of the Fomorians? What were the dragons up to? When would he see Clare again? Would she agree to marry him? When would he be able to stay with her?

He sighed and gradually drifted off to sleep. His empty belly rumbling and sore muscles aching.

CHAPTER 20 - EGAN

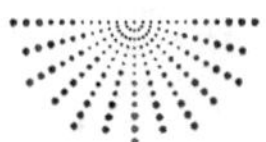

IT TOOK EGAN THREE LONG, COLD DAYS OF WALKING BEFORE he even got close to where Faerie wanted him to go. The nights kept growing colder. The snow came and went and returned again. He could feel the frozen ground through his leather boots. His pants and shirt did little to keep him warm. He should have taken warmer clothes when he left the palace. Too late now.

The meadow where he rested now was at least warmed by the sun. He brushed off a patch of snowy ground and sat down on the frozen soil to soak up some sun.

It wasn't putting out enough heat to melt the snow, so except where he'd walked, everything was covered with white. It was wet snow, crystalline when frozen. Bushes taller than a couple feet had snow on any horizontal surfaces. The view was spectacular.

A gangly, brown hare hopped into the meadow, decided he wasn't a threat and pawed through the snow to find some greenery to eat. Egan watched the creature chew what must be dried out and crunchy.

He'd spent few hours out in nature since returning to Faerie. The first several seasons, when he'd been Luminary he'd been almost exclusively in the palace. Then he'd joined in the fighting. Out in nature, but no chance to be one with it.

Which was part of being Fae. Perhaps it should be a required part of the Luminary's job—to spend time out in nature. To connect with what all of Faerie really needed and wanted.

The hare left. Slowly hopping over the hill.

Egan groaned and stood, his muscles cold from inactivity. He continued walking through the clearing. This one was long and narrow, weaving between forests bare of leaves. White, gray and brown barked trees stood like stone warriors, tall and straight.

If he'd known much about plants, Egan would have been able to say their names. Adaire would be able to. He just knew that those particular smooth barked gray ones burned hotter than the rough barked gray ones. The ones with white bark burned coolest of any of the trees he saw around here. Such was the skimpy plant knowledge of fire Fae.

The meadow seemed endless, weaving between clusters of trees. He'd never been to this part of Faerie. At least, not that he remembered. How could he have traveled the entire earth, but not all of Faerie?

There were no villages that he knew of way out here. It was just wild woodland and meadow. Home to creatures of the wild, some only found in Faerie. Here ran the fauns, the unicorns and other creatures that humans believed were only myth. And dragons, of course.

He supposed there might have been villages once. Faerie fluctuated. Fae intensely cultivated and hunted an area and then moved on to another spot. Letting the first one rest.

There were exceptions, like the area around the palace and an area in the south where grape vines were grown. They needed a very, very long time to mature and only got getter with age. Places where other crops needed some time to grow, like fruit trees and nuts besides hazelnuts. Hazelnuts grew in every hedgerow around, nuts planted and forgotten by the squirrels. Other nut trees were not so abundant.

Egan walked the length of the meadow until it ended. He was now at the foot of the mountains. They weren't tall mountains, compared to the rest of the world. They probably just barely qualified to be called that, but since they began almost at sea level, they were magnificent.

The sides facing him were smooth. Covered with grass, which looked a bit on the brown side, as it peeked out through the snow. The grassy areas looked like velvet from a distance.

As he walked closer, the mountains rose above him. At the base of one of them was a pile of rubble. As if giant boulders had tumbled down from above. It must have been a very long time ago, since there was no visible scar from the event. Nature had filled it in.

Egan began climbing the foothills. There were no trees here. He would have no fire again tonight, but Faerie clearly had a plan for him. He just wished she would tell him what it was.

He climbed up to the giant boulders at the base of the mountain. As he got closer, Egan could have sworn those boulders were intentionally placed. It wasn't in the way they looked. He felt power around them. A stone Fae would have known for sure.

Egan climbed on top of the tallest one and stood admiring the view. The woods and valleys at the center of Faerie spread out before him. She was glorious. Everything marbled in green and white. The snow sparkled in the dwindling sunlight.

Then something grabbed his leg. He was pulled down between the boulders.

Egan shot a flame at it. Something yelled, but didn't let go.

His head hit one of the rocks, as he was being dragged farther down. He fell into the darkness, losing consciousness.

CHAPTER 21 - SPIKE

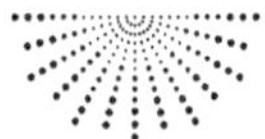

SPIKE FLEW OVER THE LEAFLESS WOODS BETWEEN THE PALACE
and the dragons' weirs for the third time, following Bluefire. The
wyvern was sure, this time, that her home was nearby.

Since the trees were bare of leaves, any movement below was
easy to see, but there wasn't much movement. Not with dragons
flying overhead. The occasional small bird flitted fearlessly
between branches, but deer remained frozen in thickets of
brambles. Hares stayed in their burrows. As did foxes and
badgers.

They landed in a clearing.

"Does any of this look familiar?" asked Spike.

"No, but it was a different time of day. The sun was going
down. The shadows were different. And there was no snow."

"It is true. Snow changes the way everything looks," said
Spike.

He was wearying of trying to find the wyvern's home. Attania
had said that others could help. Then the others had urgent
business to attend to. Attania said they would help in a few days,
but each day that passed Bluefire grew less and less sure of
where she'd flown that night.

The sylph was still sick, Attania had told him. She had nearly died. It would be some time before she would be strong enough to help retrace Bluefire's route.

"Let us go back to the dragon caves then," said Spike. "We can warm ourselves by the fire and see if there's any meat roasting." And perhaps he could catch another glimpse of that fuchsia dragon.

"Can we try just one more place? I know I can find it," said Bluefire.

"One more for today. You lead this time."

"Me, lead?"

"I have no more ideas of places to look."

"All right," she said, her voice quavering with nervousness or perhaps excitement.

She took off like a flash of lightning and Spike followed her, soon falling behind. She wove between trees. He finally gave up trying to stay with her, and rose above her. He couldn't follow her through those narrow spaces anyway. Above the tree line, he could keep pace, able to unfurl his wings completely. Bluefire finally slowed when she came to the edge of the woods and landed in a meadow.

Spike landed beside her.

"Are you giving up?" he asked.

"No. I just had to rest. I am still not a strong flyer."

"It takes many seasons of flying to become really strong. You have only had a few days."

She was panting, out of breath.

"It also helps if you slow down a bit. You will be able to fly for longer."

"I try, but I am so excited to be out in the world flying. I stood at the opening of that place I hatched for days. Wanting to go out. But too afraid."

"Perhaps you were not ready to go out those days. Maybe you were not strong enough yet."

"Maybe," she said.

The snow in this meadow was crustier, as if colder.

As soon as Bluefire had her breath back, she took off again.

Spike rose above the tree line right away this time. She flew below him, shooting between the trees like a dark, glossy shadow. These trees were still green and he had to work hard to see her beneath them.

At one point she screeched with joy. He almost laughed out loud. They stopped and flew at least three more times.

At the last stop, he said, "We need to be flying back. It will be getting dark soon."

"Just one more time," she said. "This looks like I have seen it before."

"One more time."

He was growing very tired of this, of having to take care of her. He was not meant to be a caretaker. Patience was not his gift.

He followed her again, flying above the trees until she flew out of the forest altogether and turned towards a mountain range. She flew upwards towards them.

He slowed down a bit as she flew back and forth and then around, but he kept her in sight. Finally, she landed on some rocks and folded her wings in. Seemingly stopping to breathe.

Spike landed as well, shaking out his tired wings to help them relax.

When Bluefire could breathe normally enough to speak again, she whispered, "Here."

"What?"

"Here. It is here."

"What is here?"

"Home," she said.

"Where?"

She pointed down to a hole between the rocks, that was barely visible.

"I don't think I can fit down there," he said.

There were screeching sounds coming out of the hole.

"I believe your siblings are awake. You should go down and tell them to come out."

Bluefire slithered down the hole with the speed she seemed to do everything.

Spike waited. Should he have let her go down there? Should they have come back tomorrow with another adult who could fit down that hole?

He could only get his head in, and who knew how long that tunnel was?

There was a lot of screeching going on down there. Some of it Bluefire. Was that how wyverns spoke to each other? He couldn't make any sense out of what they were saying.

The sun dropped below the trees and it began to get dark. There was no moon tonight, and it was cold here at the foot of the mountain.

Then it began to snow. Heavily.

Soon Spike was covered with white mounds of puffy snow.

And the screeching went on.

CHAPTER 22 - SOLANGE

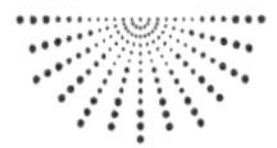

It was night when Solange opened her eyes and felt confused. She'd had another nightmare, about wyverns and Fomorians. She tried to sit up, but couldn't, and she was too hot.

But she was naked. Who took her clothes off? Where was she?

She recognized what she could see of the room while lying down. Lit only by the fireplace, the shadows of flames from the fireplace danced on the light blue ceiling. The large windows with white gauzy curtains in front of them glowed with the light of a quarter moon out in the sky. The trees beyond the window looked white. Had it been snowing?

And why was she on the narrow bed? Had she turned into Skye? No, this must be just another dream. Then Skye stood above her, the sylph's large iridescent wings fluttering with worry.

"You're awake. Let me help you sit up, so you can drink some tea."

Skye's strong arms pulled her to a sitting position almost effortlessly. She pushed pillows behind Solange's back to support her.

Her entire body felt limp and achy. She definitely couldn't

have sat up by herself. Wasn't sure if she could even stay sitting up now. Her head pounded like someone was trying to break out of it.

"Are you stable?"

Solange tried to ask what she meant but her mouth was too dry to speak.

Skye poured some tea into a stoneware mug and held it up for Solange to sip.

The tea smelled as bad as it tasted, filled with medicinal herbs. It was the same stuff she'd given to Skye to drink. It tasted like bitter green leaves and moldy dishcloths, and maybe like a three week old, never cleaned, cat litter box. She drank as much as she could anyway.

Then she could take no more and said, "Done." She couldn't even lift an arm to push it away.

"Okay," said Skye, setting the tea down. "Do you need to cough out more mucus?"

Solange shook her head.

"Your lungs don't sound as bad as they did."

"How long? Why?" asked Solange.

"You've been out at least three days. Maybe longer. When I woke up, you were out. I've been working on you. Trying to dry up the mucus."

"Thank you," said Solange. She could hardly keep her eyelids open. So tired. "Sleep now."

Skye helped her lie back down on her side, covered her up and tucked her in.

She tried to tell Skye she was too hot, but the words wouldn't come and then she was asleep again.

CHAPTER 23 - LEA

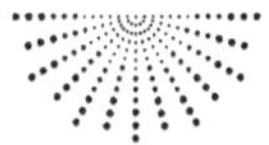

Lea walked through the snowy, oak forest. Touching the tree bark, feeling the furrows and grooves of their age. Gently brushing the lichens and mosses on the massive tree trunks as she passed. Her feet were cold and any place on her body that normally ached hurt doubly so from the snow.

Would that she were a dryad, able to curl up in a hollow of an old tree and sleep the winter away, but she wasn't. She was of the meadow plants who simply withdrew their energy into their roots deep in the earth when snow came. Lea had tried, when she was very young, maybe about Thyme's age, to dig herself deep in the earth for the winter. Her mother finally found her, near frozen, teeth chattering and body shivering. It had taken her forever to feel warm again. She hadn't done that again.

But now she was growing old, and she wanted to remain vital and alive. To heal the plants in Faerie, but what to do during the winter? The dryads who were awake generally took care of broken branches, fallen trees. They hadn't been able to keep up with the war. The battles, at least, had ceased, even if the war raged on. It was hard physical work, climbing, cutting and piling wood. Not suited for such as Lea. Hers were the small plants, not the great trees, but she had nothing to do while the plants slept.

She didn't want to sleep all winter. She'd been offered a place on the Council, but she was no policy maker.

Lea picked up a handful of snow and put it in her mouth. Crunching the ice, letting it melt in her mouth and drinking the water. She brushed off her hand and put it in her coat pocket again, to warm it.

She should go to the palace. At least see if there was a place to stay for a time. She felt out of place in all the villages. She loved her solitude, though. None of the villagers had spent season after season as a fox. She had no other shelter, had never built herself a home.

Lea continued walking through the forest, looking at deer tracks, and then those of a fox. Until finally, she came to the paved road. It was slippery beneath her soft leather boots. She walked carefully.

Just before dusk a raven startled her, or perhaps she startled it. Lea slipped and landed on her backside with a thump.

"Yowch," she yelled.

"Crawk, crawk, crawk," the raven yelled back.

"Well, you scared me too," she said, annoyed.

She got on her hands and knees to get up, and slowly stood. Now she really hurt.

She limped along through the night. It was a dark one, despite the quarter moon rising in the sky. Clouds came and went blocking it out. The snow made everything white which lit the way some, and the road was wide and easy to find. Lea walked and walked and walked. If she stopped, she'd probably freeze.

Her stomach growled. She couldn't remember how long it had been since she'd eaten. She'd had hazelnuts in her pockets, but they were all gone. Lea continued to sip snow for water. It took a lot of snow to quench one's thirst. The night wore on and then it began to snow.

She couldn't see well, but she could still feel the firmness of the road beneath her boots. Lea picked up a long straight branch someone had left leaning beside a stone marker and began to use that to poke into the snow and find which directions the road went. In the forest it was obvious. A wide clearing cut between the trees. Outside of the woods, it wasn't as clear.

The night seemed to go one forever and Lea cursed herself for her own stupidity. She should have done this sooner. When she'd first been brought back to human form, Brian had offered her a place on the council.

She'd been so confused and people so welcoming. They'd taken her back to their village and helped her heal. Given her time to get her bearings. She'd begun her work again, healing the plants. Which required traveling from village to village. She'd been too afraid to stay in one place anyway.

That would mean making true friends. She hadn't wanted to be hurt. Again. And she wasn't any good at being with other people for long periods. So she'd stayed in the forest.

It was time for her to find new work. Work that could be done in one place. Survival demanded she find it. At least in the bitter winters. She needed to learn how to live a different life.

Lea continued to walk, even when she began to stumble from exhaustion. If she didn't keep moving, she really would freeze to death. She kept changing the stick to the other hand, so she could put the coldest hand in her pocket.

It became more difficult to find the road with the stick. She could no longer feel hard stone when she stuck it through the snow. Her hands felt nothing.

Then it began to grow lighter outside. There were buildings to show where the road led. Up on the hill, the palace shimmered, crystalline in the morning sun, almost blinding her.

Lea found the steps and began to climb, falling twice, but catching herself with the stick. Then someone was at her elbow, helping her up the stairs.

"Oh dear, you are nearly frozen."

She was green. A dryad.

"Adaire. You are Adaire."

"Yes, do I know you? I can barely see you beneath all that snow."

"I am Lea. I was the fox who followed you."

"Lea! Oh my, it is good to see you. I looked for you after the gathering when you were changed back to Fae, but you had already gone. I've heard about you here and there, but our paths never crossed. What are you doing out in this weather? You look frozen."

"I am, I am … going to the palace. Been walking a long time."

"Let me carry you."

With that the dryad picked her up as if she weighed nothing, and carried her up the stairs. Lea hung on to the stick. She wanted that stick. As a reminder, in case she ever decided to be so stubbornly stupid again.

The dryad carried her to the palace doors and demanded, "Open please."

The doors swung open and then they were inside. In the entryway. The doors closed behind them.

Adaire set her down gently on a bench. Even though she was frozen, Lea could feel the pain in her rump.

Adaire said to the open air, "Please send a healer."

Then she proceeded to take off Lea's leather boots. And her snow covered coat, lying it on the bench. An earth spirit came out of the throne room.

"Oh, hello Teasel. Lea here is nearly frozen. Is there an empty room? That's warm. We need to get her unfrozen. I'm not sure if her toes are okay. Or her fingers."

The healer took one look at her toes and fingers and said, "There is a room, up the stairs and to the left, overlooking the stairs. The door is open. I will go get some supplies and hot broth."

Adaire picked Lea up again and walked up the stairs.

"Thank you."

"It's the least I can do. You kept me company during a most miserable time."

"I was lonely too," said Lea.

"I'm sure you were. Not a fox, not Fae. It's difficult being in between."

They reached the room and Lea noticed there was a fire roaring inside. She smiled as the heat touched her face.

"The couch or the bed?" asked Adaire.

"The couch is closer to the fire. But I fell on my rump and it really hurts."

"The bed for now then," said Adaire.

She set Lea down gently on the soft bed. Then shut the door so the heat would stay in.

"Let's get your clothes off and see if there's something comfy to wear in the closet. Just till you warm up again."

Lea hadn't missed that Adaire was out in the snowstorm naked and with bare feet. Dryads.

Adaire managed to get Lea's pants and shirt off without hurting her more. Then appeared with dry, warm towels and wrapped Lea in them, putting a blanket over her until the healer came up. Lea tried to ignore the pain. As she warmed up, everything hurt more. Except perhaps her hair.

She was nearly asleep when Teasel came up. The healer woke her and made her drink some sweetened tea. It tasted lovely. Mint and honey were the strongest flavors, although Lea knew there were other herbs that she should have recognized.

The healer spread a paste on her hands and feet and then wrapped them with thin cloth to keep the cream on. She examined what must be a large bruise on her backside. Lea could feel the energy flowing into it from the healer's hands.

Adaire and the healer slipped Lea into some pants and a shirt. Then lay her back in the bed.

"Sleep now until you're completely rested," said Adaire. "I'll tell Ogden and Brian that you're here, they'll send someone up to stay with you. I must go talk to the elders, but I'll stop back later today to see how you're doing."

"Thank you, Adaire."

"Again, you are very welcome. Now sleep."

And she did, hoping that her feet and hands would heal.

CHAPTER 24 ~ SKYE

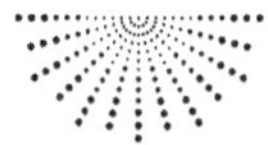

Skye paced the small, blue room, gazing out the windows at the glistening snow. The room felt too hot for her with the fire going non-stop, but Solange needed the heat.

There was too much furniture in the room. The bed, the large table and chair, the couch. It was hard to pace for long. She needed to fly and stretch out her wings. It seemed like forever since she'd flown.

Skye hadn't fully recovered from the infection. She was still coughing, but was mostly on the mend. She felt restless and trapped.

There was nothing more she could do at the moment for Solange. Skye just needed to wait for her body to heal itself a bit more. Then she'd do more energy work on Solange.

Solange's body was fighting hard against whatever it was that Plague had spat at Skye. Solange slept most of the time. When she woke, Skye tried to pour medicinal tea down her throat. That was called torturing the client. Patient rather.

Meredith had come up to speak with her as soon as she'd heard Skye was awake. Through the door, of course. No one was coming into the room until Skye was sure that any germs were dead. She wasn't quite sure how to make that happen, but would allow no one else to catch this disease if she could prevent it.

Skye told Meredith what had happened at the boundary's edge. In great detail. Meredith still didn't know what to make of it other than what Skye had felt to be true.

That the Fomorian offspring could make their powers pass though the barrier. Perhaps, even pass through themselves. The only thing that was probably stopping them from coming through was that they hadn't realized they could.

Yet.

Or that they weren't sure exactly where the boundary was. Either way it was frightening.

Meredith said the Council knew, but they hadn't made it widely known. They were grasping, trying to find a way to make the barrier completely impermeable, but that might mean no one could leave Faerie again. Ever.

Skye thought of Fiachna and Clare. Him here in Faerie, longing for her. Clare over in Glastonbury, longing for him. That would be heartbreaking if they never came together again.

She thought about herself. Skye loved helping humans, helping to heal them. All of her efforts had gone to integrate herself in the human community. To help humans heal themselves, so they could heal the earth.

She sighed and continued pacing. This time around the table. The pile of books must be for Solange. She was a reader. Skye just wasn't. But wyverns?

Skye wasn't quite sure what one was. She opened the large book on top of the pile and paged through it. There were a lot of illustrations in the book. Someone had painted pictures of them. Dragons, but with two legs. Green ones and crimson ones.

Then she turned the page. There was a painting of a blue, four-legged wyvern, and she remembered the small dragon she'd met on the road. The lost one. She'd forgotten that. Or thought it was just her own fevered dreams.

Skye folded her wings in and sat on the edge of the wooden chair and read. There was a knock at the door.

"It is Willow. I have brought up some food for you. And fresh tea for Solange."

Skye got up and walked to the door.

"Thank you Willow. I have a question. How did I get to the palace? I think I passed out down on the road. Quite a ways from here."

"Oh," said Willow. "Well, what I heard was that there was a dragon who brought you here. Little thing, she was."

"What happened to her?"

"Well Spike was here and he talked to her and then they flew off together."

"Thank you. Would you please ask Meredith if she can find out what happened to the little dragon? I would so appreciate it."

"I would be happy to, Skye. Make sure you eat while it is still warm."

"I'll get it as soon as you're down the stairs. Thank you."

Skye opened the door and brought the teapot in and set it on the table by the bed. She went back for the tray of food and closed the door, taking the tray to the table.

On a plate was a slab of chicken roasted with rosemary and thyme. And roasted potatoes, onions and carrots. Skye ate the luscious food, hungrier than she had realized. The chicken was so perfect, it nearly dissolved in her mouth as she chewed it.

Skye sat and stared at the book. When was the last time anyone had seen a wyvern? According to this book, written long before she left Faerie over a thousand years ago, no one had seen them since Faerie first came into being. Then how had one appeared to chase her and bring her to the palace?

Were they somehow related to the Fomorians? Or lived at the same time? That sounded about right.

Solange murmured, waking up.

Skye got up and helped her sit up. Then got her to drink

more tea. Solange was becoming more lucid each time she woke, but She was still too pale and weak.

After dinner Skye would work on her again.

CHAPTER 25 ~ FIACHNA

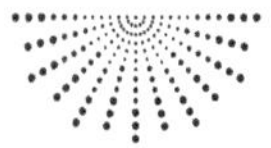

FIACHNA WOKE JUST BEFORE DAWN. HE RELIEVED ORRELL, SO the stone Fae could rest a bit. Fiachna stood next to an oak, blending in and watching the Fomorians sleep.

The weather hadn't changed. Just more snow drifting down. Even the Fomorians had stayed in place long enough to collect snow. Their fire was long out, not even smoking anymore.

The stone Fae hadn't had a fire, of course. So they were all cold, even wrapped in blankets two of them had brought along in the supply pack.

The forest was quiet this morning. Almost peaceful. Birds were silent, wary of the interlopers. Just the sound of snow falling. Which was quite a pleasant sound. If he were here under different circumstances.

Fiachna stood watch until the sun rose as high as it was going to. They were moving towards the shortest day and the sun didn't even rise above the trees at this time of year. In compensation the full moons were spectacular, high overhead, lighting up the entire land. The moon was waxing, so in a few more days, it would be full again.

Now that the day was half, over the Fomorians began to stir.

Fiachna was relieved that at least the cold and snow muffled some of their stench.

Most of the stone Fae were sitting in a hollow, below the forest level. Hidden from view. Waiting.

The Fomorians poked around their dead fire, perhaps deciding it wasn't worth trying to light it again. Then they continued moving towards the the east. Curving around the boundary of Faerie.

Fiachna didn't know exactly how the boundary worked, but most beings walking near it were convinced by Faerie that they were moving in the wrong direction. They were gently induced to move either away or along it, instead of through it. Unless one knew where the boundary was.

Fae could see the edges, as could dragons, but Fiachna was unaware of any other magical creatures who could pass through it. The boundary was impenetrable to others.

If a being was truly determined to travel in the direction where Faerie lay, it simply let them. Taking them to a piece of land that was consistent to the area. A human space, because at this point in time, humans had covered the island and left their mark everywhere. Abandoned, fouled dwellings, and overgrown, bad pastureland. Stone walls crisscrossed the island.

As the Fomorians moved down the field, Fiachna gestured to the stone Fae. Who followed him with near silence.

The Fomorians weren't silent. They argued and pushed each other around. The giants' large feet made crunching sounds in the snow.

Which woke up the birds. Who shouted warnings to each other that echoed through the entire area.

The stone Fae shadowed them all afternoon. When the sun set, the Fomorians stopped, obviously exhausted by their pitiful efforts to get somewhere. They started another fire and complained loudly to Balor about the lack of food.

"'Tis your own fault. You did na' catch any, you lazy asses," he bellowed back at them.

Fiachna took first watch. Squatting beside a yew tree which grew behind a thicket of brambles, he ate snow to get some water. Hoping it was clean snow. It was too dark to tell. It tasted clean at last.

Halfway through his watch, he stood and slowly stretched. He heard quiet footsteps behind him and looked back to see Pearce standing there. Fiachna nodded at him.

Pearce stood near him and sent, *"I spoke to the Council. We have a problem. Some of the offspring can send their magic through the barrier. Plague infected Skye, she'll be okay, but she nearly died. We don't know if they can see the boundary, or if they themselves can move through it. Clearly, their Fae blood gives them powers we didn't know they had."*

Fiachna rubbed his face with frozen snow to refresh himself and sighed deeply.

He sent, *"Thank you, Pearce."*

"You're welcome. Shall I take over?"

"You rest for now. I will call one of the others when I am done."

Pearce nodded and went to where the others sat.

Fiachna changed position, slowly. Stretching. Staring at the Fomorians.

At least it was only the offspring. They weren't as strong as the first Fomorians, but apparently they were strong enough. Despair filled his heart.

If Plague could infect Skye, Skye who was incredibly strong, what could he do to other Fae? If the offspring decided to attack humans, what would happen then?

That was what he was standing out in the snow for. To defeat the Fomorians, all of them. So Faerie was safe. And the human world too. So Faerie would open its boundaries again and he could go live with Clare.

Clare.

An image of when he'd seen her last. Standing in the darkness, up at the top of Glastonbury Tor came to him. Another image came. This one not of the past, but the present.

She was in her bedroom. Lying in bed. She stood up and

went to the window. Looked outside at the snow. And took the ring off her right hand and held it up to the stars hidden behind gray clouds.

Clare put the ring on her left ring finger and kissed it. Then crawled back into bed.

His heart nearly burst. She had made a decision. The least he could do was find a way for them to be together.

CHAPTER 26 ~ EGAN

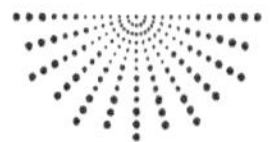

EGAN WOKE TO DARKNESS. HIS EYES GRADUALLY ADJUSTED. Fire Fae could see well in darkness. The ground beneath him was hard. The air smelled bad, from too many unwashed bodies. It felt fairly warm, which was a slight relief from the freezing snow.

His head hurt from being thumped on the rocks. He hoped it wasn't a concussion. Otherwise, he felt okay. He couldn't see anything, because he was facing a wall. Lying on broken rubble.

His clothes had been soaked from the snow and they still hadn't dried, despite the warmth here. That wasn't a good sign. It meant his fire was too low.

He heard movements behind him. They made him nervous. He was unsure what had pulled him into the hole. What lived in the earth here? Nothing he knew that could pull an adult Fae underground. Gnomes were too small.

His mind wasn't fully functioning. He'd been exhausted for too long and cold and hungry. His reserves were weak. Whatever this was, he'd better face it now. He wasn't going to get any stronger.

Egan spun around and moved to a crouched position, ready to attack whatever it was.

He found himself face to face with a small dragon. Sort of. It was red with two legs and short wings with claws just below the joint, which would function as hands. And a whiplike tail with a triangle on the tip of it. That was what had wrapped around his leg and pulled him down.

"What are you?" he asked.

The dragon cocked its head at him and whistled. Behind the dragon lay a tunnel which looked like it led to a larger cavern. This one was quite small. Egan could just barely stand up in it.

Down the tunnel came the sound of feet and he saw shadows. Three more small dragons came into the cavern, another red one and two green ones.

"Why do you live underground? You've got wings to fly, you should be outside. With the other dragons," he said, hoping conversation would help the situation.

The dragons didn't reply. But they didn't attack either.

"I'm not going to hurt you. Why don't we all go outside and you can fly. I can even take you to the other dragons if you don't know where they live."

He wasn't getting anywhere with this tactic. But he didn't think blasting them with fire was a good plan either. Even if he could summon up enough heat to ignite a fire. Which he wasn't at all sure was possible. Then there was a whooshing sound from the other cavern.

Three of the dragons ran in that direction, the fourth obviously guarding him. But the tunnel was blocked by something larger.

"You are awake," said a cheery voice. "I cannot believe how big I grew in just eight days. This tunnel is so small now. How are all of you? Have you been outside to fly yet?"

The red and green dragons didn't answer the newcomer either. They just backed into the cavern until all of them were crammed into the tiny cavern.

The new dragon had four legs and was gleaming blue-black. Larger than the others.

"Oh, what is going on here?"

"Food," said a green dragon, finally.

"No, no. That is not food. You are not food are you?"

"No," replied Egan. "I am a fire Fae."

"We wyverns do not eat creatures who can talk. That is the first thing you need to learn about being a wyvern."

Wyvern. Where had he heard of wyverns before? Egan couldn't remember.

"Why?" asked one of the green ones.

"Because if it talks, then it's not food," said the blue-black wyvern.

Egan stood watching them. The four smaller ones were gathered around the black wyvern who was easily twice their size.

"Come," she said. "You must go outside and fly. You need to learn. Once you can fly, hunting for food is easier. And my friend is outside. He is a dragon. There are hundreds of dragons where he lives and the food is very good."

"It is scary outside," said one.

"Not when you are with someone as big as Spike. He is huge."

"I know Spike," said Egan. "Is he here?"

"Yes. Come on now, let us all go out and get some fresh air," said the black Wyvern. "And then you must have names. Do you have names yet?"

"No," said a scarlet wyvern.

"I am called Bluefire, for the stars that flash through the sky. You probably haven't seen stars yet. They are beautiful. The whole world is astonishing. You will all be surprised. What adventures we will have," she said.

Egan watched as Bluefire herded the others out in front of her. He followed behind, keeping back from her whiplike tail.

"And don't be afraid of the big, black dragon. he will not hurt you. Just talk to him to show him that you are not food."

It seemed to take forever for the five of them to move

through the narrow tunnel to the larger cavern. On the far site of the larger room was the exit to the surface. There were no other rooms in this gray, limestone cave. The floor was littered with pale green broken shells from the hatchlings. There was no sign of any adult wyverns. The cave was filled with thick dust and debris that had blown in from above.

Other than the shells and fresh footprints there was no sign that any living thing had ever been here.

The wyverns scrambled up the exit easily, their bodies long and lean. Dust filled the air in the short tunnel, making Egan cough.

It took him considerably more effort to make it up. He scrambled over the rocky scree and then once in the tunnel, found enough handholds to pull himself upwards. He could smell fresh, cold air coming down from above. He appreciated the freshness, not the cold. He was far too tired.

Perhaps Spike would give him a ride to someplace warm. Egan felt sure that the wyverns were what Faerie had sent him here to discover. Why he didn't know.

Finally, he made it to the opening and pulled himself out into the light. Dwindling light though. How long had he been out? His head still ached from being cracked against the rocks. The scales on the back of his head were gashed.

The five wyverns stood in front of Spike. Looking like a flock of ducklings near their mother. He was in the process of naming them. They were looking wide eyed at the view around them.

Egan plonked down on a rock and watched them.

"You," Spike said, pointing to a scarlet one who had black shadows on her wings, "I name you Hawthorn for the scarlet black berries.

"And you," he said to the lightest green one, "I name you Birch, for the color of their green spring leaves."

To the darker green he said, "You will be named, Pine, for the gray green of the pine trees."

To the bright red wyvern he said, "I name you Yew, for the bright red berries."

The little wyverns were clearly excited.

"Oh good," said Bluefire. "Now, shall we try flying? Short distances at first. Stretch out your wings and fly over a couple of rocks and then land, feet stretched out to catch you. Watch me."

She tucked up her forelegs and flew over a couple of rocks, landing on her hind legs, like they would.

Each of the wyverns tried. They flew a bit. Two didn't land right. Rolling into crevices between the stones instead.

"It is all right. I tumbled on my first few landings too. You just get up and keep trying until you can do it. Two legs is easier to keep untangled than four, let me tell you."

After a short time, they could all land fairly well.

The sun was moving towards setting.

Spike moved closer to Egan.

"Are you all right?" he asked.

"Just very tired. And cold."

"I think we will try to take the young ones to the dragon caves tonight. It is not good for them to be here all alone. And starving. Were there any adults down below?"

"No. Nothing except egg shells. And a lot of dirt and debris. Like they'd been there a very long time. I can't remember seeing a wyvern in all my days."

"We think the eggs are ancient. The parents long dead. These young one need guidance. We have been searching for the nest for days, ever since Bluefire came to us."

"We should start for the caves now then. They can practice flying on the way. It's going to be dark soon."

"Does the dark bother you?"

"No, but the cold does."

"At least I can carry you and you can share my warmth. We will have to make many stops to rest. Even Bluefire needs to stop often."

Spike showed Egan where to sit on his back, so he could

hang onto his spikes. Egan slowly climbed up on the dragon's back, his entire body aching from the cold and shaking from exhaustion.

Then Spike told Bluefire what they were doing and that she would have to both lead the way, but fly slow enough so that the hatchlings could keep up.

"Remember how slowly you flew on your first try?"

"I will remember."

"And stop to rest in clearings that are big enough for me to land in. I will follow behind to make sure no one gets lost."

She shot straight up into the air and spun in a circle and then landed in the middle of her siblings. Telling them excitedly what was going to happen.

Then she flew off, and one by one, they followed her. Spike was clearly letting them get a ways ahead before he took off, he made up the distance quickly with his large wings.

Egan held on tightly at first, feeling the icy wind whip past his body. At least the dragon was warm beneath his lower body. Egan was able to draw the warmth up a bit into his own body and keep from freezing.

Bluefire was true to her word. She flew slowly, but they had just made it to the first group of trees when they stopped to rest.

It would be a long night. At least Spike was warming him up some. It didn't stop his head from aching though.

CHAPTER 27 ~ SPIKE

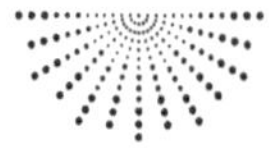

SPIKE DESCENDED AGAIN, LANDING IN A SNOWY MEADOW. THE snow made everything look so light, it was almost like daytime. The wyverns had finally learned how much space he actually took up and now left a large space open for him between them and the trees. He landed gently, taking three steps before stopping.

He was growing weary after flying most of the day. He was better at long flights, not the short hops with much landing and taking off.

The snow was old and crunchy. It had stopped falling early in the night. Which had helped him to see the wyverns down below him. In this meadow clearing, the snow came up past the top of his feet, but up to the younger wyverns' shoulders. Did it always snow this much in Faerie?

He hadn't spent a great deal of time here last winter. This was the first full winter that the dragons had spent in Faerie.

Spike slowly walked over to the wyverns. They were quiet at this rest stop. Even Bluefire seemed to have nothing to say. After having been around her for several days, he knew that was a rare thing. They were all tired, cold and hungry.

The fire Fae didn't get down off his back this time either.

Spike knew Egan was very, very cold. Yet another reason to fly slowly. Otherwise the wind would freeze him even more.

The little wyverns were huddled in a circle around Bluefire. They were getting very, very tired. Resting longer each time they stopped. The poor things had only eaten eggshells since they hatched. There had been nothing else. Until they caught Egan.

Spike was pleased he and Bluefire had arrived to find them in time. He didn't know how to express to the hatchlings what they had almost done, nearly killing a Fae. He'd leave that to the wise ones. Or a caretaker. Maybe he could leave them in the care of the fuchsia dragon. Then he could visit her often to see how the wyverns were doing. They were an unruly little bunch. Using up more energy squabbling than flying.

"How much farther?" asked Yew.

"Two more flights like the last one. With one more rest in between. Then we will be at the caves. It will be warm and there will be roasted meat. Can you make it?"

"Yes," she said. "I can fly that far. But it will be difficult."

"How about the rest of you?"

"I don't know," said Birch.

"You can do it," said Pine. "I will be right beside you."

"I will try," said Birch.

"I can fly that far," said Hawthorn.

Bluefire just opened her mouth in a grin, showing teeth. Spike had had no doubts about her.

It was like he said, two more short flights and as the sun rose, the mountain containing the dragon caves loomed closer.

The wyverns were spurred on by Spike moving towards the front as they cleared the last clump of woods. Bluefire raced out ahead, shooting straight for the mountain. Her siblings forming a green and red stream behind her, flapping their short little wings madly.

Spike circled, letting them land first.

Few dragons were up and outside this early, but the fires

were built and Spike could smell meat roasting. He groaned as the scent wafted to him.

The little ones all landed. Some tumbled a bit on the hard surface. Then they got out of the way so he'd have room to land.

He set down and walked over to one of the fires. Egan climbed off his back and walked directly into the fire. The dragons nearby, Spike included, inhaled in fear. Egan stuck his head back out.

"I seem to have forgotten my manners. It's all right isn't it? If I share your fire to warm myself?"

"You are welcome," said Spike. "I do not think any of us have ever seen a Fae do that."

"I'm a fire Fae. I was born in fire. Fire heals me. It is my element." Then Egan's head vanished into the flames and it looked as if he'd never been there.

Spike tore some meat off a carcass and handed it out to the wyverns. They ate hungrily, staring at the new dragons.

Finally, Yew paused and said, "You will not eat us will you? All of us can talk."

"We will not eat you," said Attania, who was adding wood to the fire. "Not any of you."

Yew returned to eating.

Once Spike finished eating, he said to Attania, "I must go sleep. Will someone take these youngsters to where the hatchlings sleep when they have finished eating. They need to rest. And then they need to learn."

"I will see to it," she said, pulling more meat off the carcass and giving it to the wyverns.

As Spike walked past the fire, a fire tender tossed more wood on it and shot a blast of fire at the flames. As they often did.

From within the fire Egan roared, "Oh, that feels wonderful! Please do it again!"

Startled, the fire tender shot another blast of flames towards the fire.

"Thank you!" he yelled.

Spike chuckled and moved slowly towards the hallway that led to the large sleeping chamber, his full belly making him drowsy.

If he lived forever, he didn't think he could ever learn enough about Fae.

CHAPTER 28 ~ SOLANGE

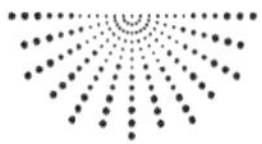

SOLANGE WOKE TO DAYLIGHT. SUN STREAMED THROUGH THE window, low in the sky like it always was during the winter. The light bright and blinding. There was noise outside in the hallway. People talking, they sounded happy.

She lay looking up at the boring ceiling. Why didn't ceilings ever get decorated in bedrooms? After all, people woke up every morning to the ceiling. Was a plain light blue ceiling really the best that the palace could do? Was it supposed to make one feel contemplative?

Solange wasn't feeling contemplative. She felt weak and cranky.

At least she could breathe. Hell, at least she was alive. She heard movement and then saw Skye coming towards her.

"You're awake again. Good, let me pour you some more tea."

"Please, anything but that awful tea."

"You must be feeling better. You're hardly at all. Do you want to sit up?"

"Yes."

Skye helped her to a sitting position.

Solange's arms felt limp. She could barely raise them.

"How long have I been like this?"

"Maybe a week."

"That long? How is Dylan?"

"He seems fine. He's been here at least twice a day, every day. Asking about you. I haven't opened the door. I don't know how long these germs live. I don't want anyone else infected."

Solange nodded.

"Would you like some food? I still have some beef and barley soup left."

Solange nodded, which was easier than talking.

The soup was thick and satisfying. The beef gave it a strong flavor and the barley filled her up quickly. She didn't have more than a few spoonfuls.

"So, what's new?" asked Solange, finally. Feeling desperate to be diverted from how sick she felt.

"Not much. There was a massive snowfall. It's still around, but beginning to melt. It came up to my hips. Everyone pretty much stayed where they were. Oh, but in the middle of the storm Lea arrived, half frozen. You remember, the Fae who the Fomorians turned into a fox."

Solange nodded.

"So, she's here. And Adaire's back. She's been off in the forest, but felt the storm coming on, so she came back to be with Tuuli. Egan's disappeared."

"How?"

"Don't know. He reported in one morning to the Council, then left his cloak in the entryway and just walked off. My bet is that he's finally come to his senses and is off looking for Lassair. In the middle of this huge storm. Silly fire Fae. Hope he found a nice warm fire and stays there for the rest of the winter."

"Meredith? Aura?"

"Meredith has come here twice a day, worried sick about you. She and Aura are spending all their time in the library, trying to sort out the Fomorian problem."

"And I'm not there to help them."

"No, you're not, so get well, you slacker," said Skye.

Solange laughed and said, "I could use some crappy tv to watch about now."

"Yeah, Faerie's way behind on the crappy tv thing. Sometimes I'd even like to watch it. I do have a TV though."

"Where?" She didn't believe Skye.

"In Glastonbury. In storage. When I had to leave in such a hurry, I asked Clare to put all my stuff in storage."

"Lot of good it does there," said Solange.

"Yeah well, it wouldn't do any good here, either. No electricity. No cable or satellite. No internet, but I'll tell you what. When you're well, and this whole Fomorian thing's blown over, and Faerie's open again, I'll take you back to Glastonbury with me and we can break out the tv."

"By then I won't want it."

"Not my fault," teased Skye.

"I need a bath," said Solange. "I stink."

"Yes, you do, but give yourself another day. You're still pretty weak. I don't think you can walk yet."

"Yeah, you're right. I'm getting tired again. Five minutes of eating and conversation and I'm toast."

"It'll get better."

Solange sighed. Skye helped her roll over and sleep on her other side.

She was ready to be well, and get back to work helping Meredith and Aura.

She'd always hated being sick.

CHAPTER 29 ~ LEA

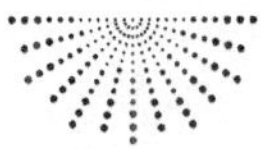

Lea slept for hours upon hours. It was evening when she woke up the first time. She quickly went back to sleep, feeling warm and comfortable for the first time in days. Then when she woke again, it was daytime.

She scratched her face with her bandaged hand. When would she be able to take the bandages off? Her fingers didn't hurt, at least.

Her hair had been oiled, brushed and neatly braided, to keep it out of her way while she slept. The healer? What was her name? Teasel, that was it.

Lea snorted. Whoever had brushed it must have been very, very patient. There had probably been birds nesting in her hair. Getting the tangles out just hadn't seemed important lately. Maybe never. She should just cut it and be done with it, but she liked her long hair.

Lea gingerly moved to sit up. The place she'd fallen on her rump hurt when she moved. It caused the surrounding area to ache as well. But nothing hurt as much as everything had during the last part of her trip to the palace.

The room around her was made completely of wood and felt cosy. A fire had been built in the fireplace, which accounted for the warmth in the room. Spring green curtains hung on both sides of the large window, leaving it open to a view of the white landscape outside. Massive, wide and tall oak trees rose up past the window. Obviously, growing downhill from the palace.

Oaks were a good tree for that. In the summer they would provide shade, keeping the room cool. Now in the winter, they let the sun stream in, adding warmth to the room.

It was furnished sparsely with the large bed and a big table nearby. Over by the fire sat three comfortable looking chairs and a low table.

Lea had never lived indoors for more than a night or two. She could live in a room like this. It was plain, but beautiful. There was only one decoration. On one wall hung a collection of dried seedpods from various plants, entwined with interesting branches. Whoever put it together was an artist with an appreciation of the seasons and plants.

She slid her legs off the bed to touch the floor. At the same time, the door to the room opened and an earth Fae carrying a tray walked in.

"Oh, you are awake. Stay on the bed so I can look at your feet before you get up."

Lea lifted her legs back onto the bed. The motion made her wince.

"Your backside hurting you?" asked the Fae, who must be a healer, setting the tray on the bedside table.

"Yes."

"Well, I will do some more work on that. And I brought up another salve. I did not want to wake you to put it on earlier. Seemed to me that you needed your sleep."

"That I did. What is your name? Are you Teasel?"

"No, I am Willow."

The healer held up Lea's left leg and began to unwrap the bandages. Once unwrapped, Lea's skin looked red, but everything felt okay. She wiggled her toes.

"This foot will be fine. It got just a bit burnt from the cold. We Fae are hardy folk."

Then the healer unwrapped her other leg and both her hands.

"You will be fine. I will find some soft socks for your feet. You are to wear them until the redness leaves your skin. And we will put more salve on before you put the socks on. You are not to go outside until it warms up."

"But that will be spring." Lea couldn't imagine staying inside till spring.

"Well, at least till there is no frost on the ground, and definitely no snow."

"I can live with that, but where will I stay?"

"Here," said Willow, gesturing around at the room.

"This grand room, all for me?"

"Yes. The palace created this room for you. She wants you to stay and be comfortable."

Had anyone ever wanted her to stay and be comfortable? Lea couldn't remember such a thing.

Willow had her lie down and roll over. Then she used energy to work on the bruise.

Lea could feel the heat moving across her entire backside. Willow worked on Lea for quite a while. Lea would have been content had it been forever. The healer made her feel wonderful.

When she'd finished, Willow said, "You are very bruised. It will heal, but you can expect to be sore. So move slowly."

"I feel so sleepy now, I do not think I will be moving anytime soon."

"Good. There is nothing calling you. Rest and let your body heal. I will leave a covered bowl of soup for you on the table. You can eat when you wake again."

Lea felt a blanket covering her back up and she fell back asleep.

CHAPTER 30 ~ SKYE

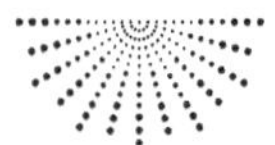

Skye stood at the closed, blue painted door of the room, talking to Meredith, who was on the other side. She longed to get out of the room, but it was too soon. Solange was only just now able to get out of bed. Skye still tired easily.

She'd paced every inch of floor, working on getting her strength up. Doing exercises and stretches for her wings, trying to keep them from getting any weaker. Mostly she lay or sat around, feeling like a limp balloon that had lost most of its air.

Skye had also lost track of time and Meredith hadn't been paying very close attention either. Skye decided they wouldn't leave the room until it had been at least three weeks since Solange got sick. She had no idea what Plague had spit at her, but she wanted to take no chances with infecting anyone else with it. So far no one else had gotten sick.

Meanwhile, the small room was making her crazy. She longed to get out and fly.

The room stank like two sick people lived there. When they were both warm enough they opened the windows for a time, trying to air it out, but it was too cold outside to leave the windows open for long.

There was a shower in the room, which was good. Otherwise the place would have smelled worse.

Skye didn't know what herbs the healers had put in the tea, but she hoped to never encounter the concoction again. Would she ever get that bitter awful smell out of her nose, or her skin?

She and Solange had already used up all their conversation. They'd talked about wyverns. And Fomorians. About Dylan. And the state of the human world. And about how Skye wanted to get back to Glastonbury. They'd talked about everything except the weather and heaven help them if it came to that.

So Skye stood by the door, the wood floor cooling her bare feet, hoping that Meredith could tell her something which would occupy her mind, for a least a little while.

"I believe that Spike took the wyvern back to the dragon caves," said Meredith

"Could you find out for me? I'd like to know where it went."

"Certainly."

"Had you ever seen a wyvern before?"

"No, and I barely saw this one either. I was still sleepy and I was paying more attention to you."

"Have you seen any of the books sent up by the library?"

"I wasn't aware the library sent books up to you."

"I think they were for Solange. I don't know. Anyway, they're all about wyverns, and how ancient they are. They lived mostly around the time the Fomorians ruled this area. And they're venomous, like snakes. I don't know if these eggs were from that time or more recent. The wyvern said there were four other unhatched eggs, but it was the only one that hatched so far. There were no adults around. So where did the adults go?"

"That's an interesting question. I'll speak with Dylan and have him call for Spike. I'll make sure to find out what happened."

"Thank you. And warn Spike that they're venomous. The one I met was very young and immature. Only a few days old. They may not know about the venom. So it needs to be warned not to bite anyone, even in play."

"I'll pass that on."

"Has Egan shown up yet?"

"No, not yet. I'm sure he's fine. He just needs time alone, I'd guess."

Skye wished Meredith was being more forthcoming.

"So, any other news?"

"No, the Council is just discussing what needs to happen if winters like this one continue. Some of the elders are having a difficult time of it."

"Oh," said Skye.

"And it's time for me to go back to the discussion. I wish I had some exciting news for the two of you. Ask the palace for some entertainment. She may come up with something."

"Thanks Meredith," said Skye, walking away from the door and pacing around the room again.

Solange sat on the couch, staring into the fire and looking as if she were about to fall asleep again.

"Why don't you go back to bed?" asked Skye.

"I thought if I were out of bed that I'd be able to stay awake for more than two minutes."

"Apparently not," said Skye. "Do you need help?"

"Yes, probably. I'm not too steady yet," said Solange.

Skye helped her up and walked Solange back to the bed. Solange was still really wobbly. It took a lot of effort for her to climb up onto the bed. She was out of breath.

Skye went back to the couch to get the comforter for her.

"Well, at least your lungs are getting a workout," said Skye, smoothing the comforter over Solange.

"Yeah, I guess there really is a bright side to all this," she said, sarcastically.

Skye laughed, "We really are a pair. Please don't ever let us be sick at the same time again."

Solange was already asleep by the time Skye stopped laughing.

Skye went to the window and stood looking out. The area behind the palace where the fountains usually ran was completely empty. No Fae out enjoying the snow. No one flying or walking.

It was almost as if no one else existed.

Skye sighed and went back to sit at the table, looking at the books again and trying to read the text that Solange had helped her decipher. This was important or else the library wouldn't have sent the books up.

But why?

CHAPTER 31 ~ FIACHNA

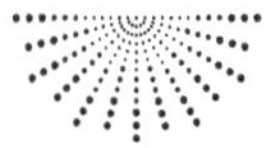

Fiachna and Pearce watched the Fomorians cross the river. Balor waded across the wide, but currently shallow river. Corb floated almost effortlessly across it. Cethlenn the fog drifted across obscuring their view. Elatha and Dela waded across. And Conand blew himself across.

It was midday and the sky was clear again. Crisp and cold.

Fiachna had sent all the other stone warriors far into the interior woods to hunt for game and cook it. And warm themselves by a fire and eat. Then to catch up with him and Pearce and bring the cooked meat.

In exchange he and Pearce got all the blankets.

Fiachna wasn't sure it was a fair trade. He wouldn't have relished all the extra walking, but the ones who went were all young. They'd enjoy the challenge.

As soon as the Fomorians were well away from the river, behind brush and headed east at a good pace, Fiachna and Pearce removed their clothes and boots, and wrapped everything in blankets. Holding the bundles above their heads, they waded across the frigid river inside Faerie. The giants had an advantage. The water came up to Fiachna's shoulders. The rocks in the river were sharp on his feet, but his feet were hard from a long lifetime of walking. Sometimes in boots, mostly barefoot.

On the other side of the river, they dried off with blankets and dressed again, trying to keep the snow out of their boots. Then they took off walking quickly to catch up to the Fomorians.

Fiachna led the way behind a hedgerow of hazels and dog roses. There were other plants, but he couldn't recognize them just from their twigs. If they were leafed out, he might have known their names.

He heard bellowing and decided they were close to the Fomorians. There was also a great deal of yelling. They came to the edge of a forest. There was just enough of a thicket of bushes for them to hide behind and watch.

Balor was bellowing at another Fomorian. Fiachna realized that the other one was Muir. So they'd caught up with the Fomorian offspring, too. Balor and Muir were pushing each other around. Muir was just as tall and strong as Balor. The other offspring stood off to the side looking angry. Plague was among them.

None of Balor's group showed much emotion. It was just another fight to them, but it was clear the offspring felt differently.

Balor roared, "Ya said ya wanted no part of my revenge. Then why are ya still here? Trying to steal my land right out from under me?"

Muir yelled, "It's not your land, you old shit. And it never will be. We know how to defeat them. You're too stupid to figure out how."

His voice sent chills up Fiachna's spine.

The offspring had a plan. Along with size, power and intelligence. Intelligence, something the Fomorians had always lacked and it always stopped them from conquering Faerie.

"Well, tell it to me then if yer so smart."

"No. We don't want to defeat them."

"Ya don't have a plan, ya bloody coward. Yer no kin of mine."

At that Muir shot a blast of water knocking Balor off his feet.

Enraged Balor pummeled Muir to the ground. Balor walked away. His back to Muir, showing complete contempt. Balor raised his fists in triumph.

A stupid move by one who underestimates his opponent. Then again, no one ever really challenged Balor.

Muir stood again and attacked. Stronger than before.

As if he was not hurt at all.

Balor went down again. Yelling something unintelligible. He got back up. And flattened Muir again.

"Attack me while my back's turned will ye?

With that he ripped off his bandanas and opened his baleful eye.

Muir slid across the grass trying to escape its gaze.

Then Lightning stepped forward, blasting Balor directly in his third eye with a lightning bolt as powerful as any Fiachna had ever seen.

Balor fell. Screeching in anger or pain. Fiachna couldn't tell.

Then Ùisdean, of the stone islands, moved to Muir. Helping him up. The two of them walked away. Towards the east. Followed by Àed, the volcano, Hurricane, Blizzard and the other offspring. Lightning turned and followed them.

Only Plague stayed behind with the original Fomorians. No one went to help Balor. Not one of them wanted to look at his baleful eye.

There was bloody snow all around Balor. He packed it into the wound and just sat on the ground. Not broken. Fiachna didn't bother to hope for that, but the giant was temporarily fettered.

Fiachna was left wondering if the eye was damaged permanently.

Balor would try it soon, he knew. He wouldn't be all right with not knowing. But even without the eye, the giant was still formidable. He'd just keep on coming until something stopped him.

Fiachna hoped to see the day that happened.

Soon.

CHAPTER 32 ~ EGAN

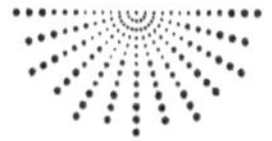

EGAN STAYED IN THE DRAGONS' FIRE FOR DAYS UPON DAYS, luxuriating in the heat. Especially whenever one of them blasted the waning fire with their own. Why had he never discovered dragon fire before? He hadn't heard of it from other fire Fae either. That was probably a good thing.

Because then he truly might never leave the flames.

He sustained himself by picking pieces of meat off the deer carcasses that shared the fire with him. He felt himself renew. His power returned with the intensity of the heat. He cleaned and shined his scales, using the scant fat dripping from the carcasses to oil them to a shiny gloss.

His scales had grown, now completely covering the tops of his feet and rising up towards his knees. In no time his skin would be completely covered with them.

When he finally stepped out of the fire, he looked and felt like a new Fae. He could even stand the cold wind, whipping through the cave which was open on two sides.

Many dragons were nearby eating and probably hadn't realized he was in the fire. His sudden appearance seemed to surprise them.

"Egan," said Ethelgarde bowing at him.

"Good evening. Or is it morning?"

"Morning," said the massive dragon, who was the color of flashing opals. A rainbow of light.

"How is it going with the wyverns?"

Ethelgarde snorted a sort of laugh.

"They are more trouble than all the other hatchlings together."

"They seemed that way to me."

"They will be fine, I believe, but they are a challenge. Being on their own for so long after they hatched was not good for them."

"Where are the adult wyverns? I saw no sign of them in the cave. It looked like the eggs had been there for a very long time."

"We do not know. Few of us even remembered the old tales of Wyverns. Fewer had seen one. Let alone a clutch of five. They are ill-tempered, snarly and their bite is venomous. Luckily, we learned that before one of them bit anyone. I do not know how we will keep them from biting. Young dragons often bite during play."

"Perhaps it was not a good thing to bring them here."

"It would have been cruel to leave them where they were. Without food, other than shells? Without guidance or protection? Spike told me the four younger ones were very frightened."

"I believe they were," said Egan. What did wyverns need to be protected from? He couldn't think of a single thing that could have been successful attacking them. Except humans or Fomorians. The wyverns were inside Faerie. Perhaps they eggs were laid before Faerie had been closed.

Could they possibly be that old?

"You and Spike had no choice, but we will need to watch them carefully."

"Where is Spike?"

"He is likely sleeping. He was out all day alone yesterday. Hunting."

"All day alone? Is that usual?"

Ethelgarde laughed again. "Bluefire idolizes him and follows him around. The other wyverns follow her around, when they can. Which makes Spike the unfortunate receiver of most of their attention. He has never wanted to be a caretaker for young dragons."

Egan shook his head. He loved children. He'd loved Lassair's daughter Aine, although he hadn't been able to spend as much time with her as he'd liked. Being Luminary had taken nearly all his time.

One of the things Lassair had said before she left was that Aine deserved more than just his passing attention. She'd been right. Fae children were scarce and therefore precious. He should have handed the job of Luminary over to the Council sooner, but regrets would not help him live his life.

"You seem sad, fire Fae."

"I am sad. I have lost the love of my life. She left the palace some time ago. To return to her village. I have searched and searched, yet cannot find it. When Spike found me I was so depleted, I could barely fight off baby wyverns. I cannot go out in the snow again and search for her. Yet I must find her."

"Could I be of assistance?"

"How?" asked Egan.

"I feel a need to stretch my wings today. The sun is out, it is warmer today. Come for a ride on me and we shall search for her village. If you do not find it, you will at least be assured of a good meal and a hot fire when you return here. Then tomorrow, I am sure another dragon will need to go flying."

Egan looked at the huge dragon.

"I have no words to thank you enough."

"Your intention is enough. Would you like to fly with or without rigging?"

Egan walked around to the side of the large dragon.

"I think with some help, I could climb up and then hang onto the flap of skin at the base of your neck."

"All right then. Climb on up."

The dragon bent his elbow so the front of his body was lower. Egan scrambled up using the dragon's forearm and upper arm as footsteps. And the bone at the front of the wing. Then he was up, sitting on the dragon.

"Ready?"

"Ready."

Ethelgarde slowly turned and walked towards the edge of the cliff.

And then dove.

CHAPTER 33 ~ SPIKE

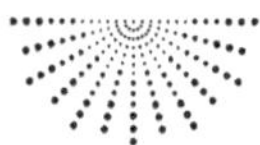

Spike slept through breakfast and dinner. He never did that. But he was tired of the wyverns. Sleeping or flying off by himself seemed to be the only way to avoid them.

Hatchlings were not allowed in here. The massive common cave where the adult dragons slept. It was just a normal cave, occasionally freshened in the spring, summer and fall by a few dragons who would gather and bring in fragrant dried grasses for those who wished it, for them to sleep on.

Spike tried to go to listen to the wise ones after eating the other night, but had been waylaid by Bluefire, and of course she had been followed by all the others.

His plan to check on their progress with the fuchsia dragon had not worked. She was in charge of a group of older hatchlings. Another dragon entirely was caring for and teaching the wyverns, and the wyverns hated that dragon.

When Spike was near him, they did nothing but complain about their caretaker, Ragwort. The problem was that ever since the caretaker was told they were venomous, he'd been afraid of them. They were smart enough to figure that out and used it against him.

The wyverns were individuals, but even Spike had to admit,

they had habits and family traits that were not easy to get along with. Were they supposed to be solitary creatures? Their manners and the disappearance of the adults led him to think that, but they seemed to thrive on being together. Bluefire was the only one he ever saw alone. Then again, she was the only one who had four legs. She looked more like a normal dragon, and she'd hatched first with no one around. She was also less mean than the others.

Spike groaned and got to his feet. He was hungry. He hoped the wyverns were either with their caretaker, learning good manners, or sleeping.

He went down the tunnel to the open cavern, smelling roast goat. His giant stomach rumbled loud enough to cause a landslide. There were few dragons there and it was light out. He hoped again that the wyverns were at their lessons.

Spike ate his fill of the roast meat, barely tasting it. Wind whipped through the area today, blowing smoke everywhere.

He thought again of the fuchsia dragon. He should give up on ever meeting her. He should find someone else. Spring would come and once again he would have no mate. A lonely, dull scaled black dragon.

His fire would never come in.

He flew off the edge of the cliff, heading towards the ocean. By the time he got there it would be dinnertime. He could fill up on raw fish and then head home, returning long after the wyverns would have been wrangled back into the sleeping area.

The air was fairly warm and fresh from days of snowfall.

It was a wonderful day for flying and he meant to enjoy it.

CHAPTER 34 ~ SOLANGE

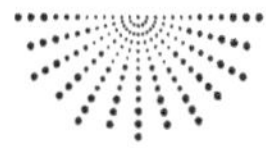

SOLANGE SHOWERED IN THE OPEN BLUE AND WHITE TILED area of the room. The palace had provided a liquid lavender soap for hair and bodies. No conditioner though.

She dried off and put on fresh clothes that the palace found for her. Black pants, a yellow ochre shirt and tan boots. Then she sat in one of the straight backed, wooden chairs and brushed her long hair getting the snarls out.

Skye showered second and brushed her knee length hair, twisting it into one long braid. And of course, she was naked.

Skye's nudity didn't bother Solange. It was just that the sylph was naked in such a cold room. It was still freezing out and most of the palace wasn't that warm. It made Solange shiver, just looking at her. Most Fae had little problem with cool temperatures. Skye and Dylan were no exception.

"Hurry up," said Skye.

"I'm hurrying. How do you do your hair so fast?"

"Millennia of practice."

Solange shook her head.

They were getting out today. Three weeks were up. They were leaving this room and the healers were coming in to clean further. To make sure the disease was dead. Using whatever magic healers used to do such things. They would make sure that no one else would get infected.

Ever.

Solange wouldn't wish this on anyone. Even the Fomorians. She finally got the last tangle out of her hair and set the brush down.

"What about the books?" Solange asked.

"The palace will take care of them."

"I thought everything in this room was to be burned."

"Not the books. I'm not that daft. I asked the palace to put them somewhere very cold and dry for several months. Then someplace very hot for several months, but not so hot they'd burn or be destroyed. And then to be returned safely to the library."

"I sure hope this disease is dead."

Skye said, "So do I."

Solange opened the door. Dylan stood outside, a pool of water at his feet indicating he'd been waiting a while.

He rushed forward and hugged her.

"I've missed you so." Then he kissed her with a sweet tasting kiss so long and deep that it made her head spin.

"I missed you too." And she had. Solange hadn't forgotten those dark green-black eyes that made her want to dive inside him and plumb the depths of his mysteries.

"Where's my welcome party?" asked Skye.

"Downstairs, I believe. In the throne room. For both of you. I just wanted to get my kiss in first."

Skye was first down the stairs, her wings out and fluttering.

Solange knew Skye had been planning on going flying, first thing. It looked like she'd have to wait a bit.

She and Dylan followed Skye down the stairs. He held firmly onto her arm, which was probably a good thing. She wasn't afraid to walk, but wasn't sure of herself on the stairs. Not yet. Still, she felt a dozen times better than she had last week, when she could barely wobble across the room.

There was a lot of noise coming from the throne room.

Solange and Dylan followed Skye inside. The large, airy room was decorated with garlands of greens and red berries. Fires blazed in the five fire pits. The room was half full of Fae There were musicians which was unusual for breakfast. The smell of food nearly knocked Solange flat.

Everyone shouted, "Happy Yule!"

Skye's mouth dropped open.

"Is it Yule already? Well, then it really is time to celebrate."

"We thought you knew," said Aura. "And that was why you decided to come out of the sickroom today. So we decided to make it a celebration worth remembering."

Aura stood back to reveal a view of a table laden with food.

The sight of it made Solange's mouth water. She hadn't eaten breakfast this morning, looking forward to eating down here. She was tired of bowls of cooked oats. Bowls of soup. Bowls of stew.

She walked closer to the table and picked up a plate. Dylan took it for her and held it over near the food, motioning for her to load it up. She took a flaky looking pastry, some sausages and cooked eggs. And another pastry that looked like a cinnamon roll, but she didn't think Faerie had cinnamon.

"I'll start with that," she said.

Dylan carried the plate over to a table. Solange followed him and managed to climb over the bench without falling over. Meredith came and sat by them, her plate not quite so full of food.

A kitchen Fae came by with mugs of mulled wine. Which smelled of cinnamon. So, of course Faerie had cinnamon, but where from? And could they get chocolate? She'd die for a piece of chocolate.

"No thank you," said Solange to the kitchen Fae. "It's a bit early for me. I'll stick with tea."

Dylan poured her a cup. It smelled dark and spicy.

She ate the sausages first, listening intently to other's

conversations. She had missed this so. Everyone eating together, and hearing what everyone was up to, and of course the wonderful choices of food. Communal meals were one of the things that made her love Faerie the most.

That, and Dylan.

CHAPTER 35 ~ LEA

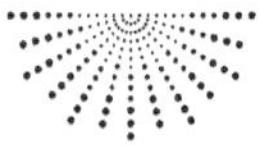

Lea came downstairs for the Yule feast that evening. She'd never enjoyed parties, but it was time to give it a try. The throne room was strung end to end with pine boughs entwined with red glass berries. The tables filled with exotic food, like chocolate and oranges.

A group of Fae played and sang by the fire. The sweetest music she'd ever in her life heard. A fiddle, a drum and a tin whistle. Later on someone played the Uilleann pipes. And much later, a guitar. Some of them were human instruments, but in the hands of Fae, it just didn't matter. Fae made music their own.

Adaire came up and dragged Lea over to sit with her and Tuuli. Which was nice. There were other Fae at the table, not all earth spirits. They made her feel at home with their lively chatter.

She had one cup of mulled wine. That was enough to make her feel it. She rarely had a chance to drink alcohol.

"Oh Lea, tomorrow some of the dragons are going to come and get us. To take us to see the hatchlings. Will you come?" asked Adaire.

"I am not supposed to go out in the snow and cold."

"Well, the snow is gone. We could bundle you up to keep you

warm. It is cold flying on a dragon. Shall we ask the healer if you'll be all right? The dragons will have warm fires when we get there."

"Yes, let us ask Willow. I would like to see my friend Silver."

"I have met Silver," said Tuuli. "She is an amazing dragon. I have never heard such stories."

"I am sure she has remarkable stories. I have never met anyone with such a zest for life," said Lea.

Adaire went to Willow's table and told her about Lea's desire. Willow followed her back to where Tuuli and Lea sat.

Willow said, "Adaire says you would like to go visit the dragons tomorrow."

"Yes, I really would."

Willow picked up Lea's hands and looked at them.

"How do your feet look? Has the redness left them as well?"

"Yes, my feet look just like normal."

"And your bruise?"

"It still hurts a bit if I move the wrong way."

"Well, I think it will be fine. It is just a short trip. But you must dress very warmly. Gloves, fur boots, hat, leather pants and shirt, fur jacket."

"Goodness, will I even be able to move?" asked Lea.

"You will. You cannot get cold again until next winter."

"I understand. I will dress warmly."

"All right then, you can go."

"Thank you. Oh, this will be fun," said Lea.

The rest of the evening continued to be wonderfully festive. The Council members each made a speech about the prosperity of Faerie and their hopes for the future.

Of course, little mention was made of the war, the standoff.

Then Meredith picked up a very small chunk of wood, the remains of last year's yule log and tossed it into the fire. The flames blazed as if a bucket of pine needles had been tossed in.

Perhaps there was a bit of magic going on, but Lea wasn't going to say a thing about it.

It was the best Yule she'd ever celebrated.

At the end of the night, Adaire and Tuuli, sweet spirits that they were, helped her climb back up the stairs.

In her room, Lea slipped off her soft socks, green pants and tunic. Then slid into the bed, watching the full moon out the window. The long night moon. She fell asleep dreaming about the morrow.

She was going to see dragons.

CHAPTER 36 ~ SKYE

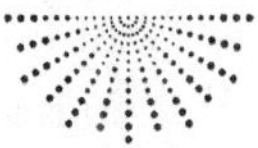

After breakfast Skye felt tired, but she'd been trapped inside too long to put off flying.

She put her dishes on a cart and then surveyed the bustling throne room. It seemed that despite the cold, Fae were coming out to celebrate Yule. The snow had mostly melted.

Most Fae had had to hold their own private Solstice celebrations just a few days earlier, according to Aura. The snow had just been too deep.

Skye decided to forego flying up to one of the four sylph's entrances. Platforms up near the ceiling to land on or fly off of which led to a similar platform on the outside of the palace, with a doorway in between. Making it easy for sylphs to enter the palace without having to open and close doors while dealing with folding in their wings. It also made the main entryway less crowded.

If she was going to fall flat on her face from having weak wings, she'd rather do it in a less crowded spot. So she walked out the main entrance to the near empty courtyard and then around back where the fountains and pools lay. The back of the palace was unoccupied.

She took off down a path through the oak grove, flapping her wings. It took some time before she gained any altitude, but Skye decided she felt strong enough to keep going once she got above the tree line.

It wasn't too cold for her and she soared through the crisp air. Not as fast as normal, but fast enough. The sky was clear which made it a bit cooler, than with cloud cover. The sun streamed through the leafless oaks to the forest floor below.

She made a wide circle around the palace and flew off towards the dragons' caves. Passing over woodland and clearing, then over the lake. It looked still and quiet, with ice around the edges. The water Fae were still down deep, sleeping or telling stories. Celebrating Yule in their own fashion.

More forest streamed past as Skye flew. She spotted a small herd of deer, out in a meadow. Grazing on dried grasses and anything else they could find at this time of year. The farther she flew the stronger she felt.

How she had missed flying. Whenever she couldn't fly for a time and then returned to it, she did so with profound gratitude. Flying made her feel so free from constraints. Made her remember the times she spent hiding from Fomorians, stuck inside a human body she'd created.

Skye closed her wings and spun in a spiral, still shooting forward. Then opened her wings and flapped them, feeling her own power.

As she passed around a woodland of ancient, tall yews, the dragons' mountain came into view. It was a beautiful, perfectly cone shaped mountain. A volcano that hadn't blown its top off. At least not yet.

She grew closer and saw the outdoor section of the cave crowded with dragons. She'd only been there a few times since they moved back to the caves. It must be midday, not a time when it was normally crowded. Were they celebrating too?

Some of the dragons saw her coming and made space for her to land. Skye landed, folding in her wings. She was winded, but not enough to worry her. The dragons in front of her opened up a path so she could move to the front of the crowd and see. In the front, against the intricately painted cave wall stood Attania, a beautiful dragon with scales the color of sapphires.

She was addressing the crowd of dragons, who were all adults.

"So, that is the problem. We must find a caretaker who the wyverns will respect. One who can restrain them and teach them what they need to know to live. It may be that they will never fit into our community, but they must be taught to hunt and survive. If it is true that they are better suited to be solitary, then they desperately need this. We need to do this today. We cannot have another accident like this."

Keirosum spoke, "I agree with you, Attania, but given all that, who is willing to care for them? And risk one of them escaping and biting another hatchling? I would not want to be responsible for another accident."

Attania said, "That is a good point, but you would not be responsible. We can only do so much. Unless there are five caretakers. And even then, we need to sleep. What we need is several of us willing to take on this task. Otherwise, things will get worse. If they are not taught now while they are young, what will the wyverns be like when they are older?"

An yellow and orange dragon Skye didn't recognize spoke next, "What all of you must realize is that they are not like our hatchlings. Ours are born knowing little and then learning. The wyverns appear to be born with knowledge. Maybe even fully formed. I am not sure they can be taught."

"I agree Ragwort, perhaps they are meant to be solitary," said Attania. "We still need to teach them to hunt and survive."

"Do we?" asked Maximus. "I do not think we do if it means exposing us, and especially our precious hatchlings, to risk."

Attania had spotted Skye.

"Welcome Skye. As you can see we are having a crisis."

"Happy Yule," said Skye. "What has happened?"

"One of the wyverns picked a fight with one of our

hatchlings and then bit his tail. It is possible the hatchling may lose his tail, may even die. It is not clear yet," said Attania.

"May I be of assistance? I am a healer."

"I am sure our healers would be pleased to consult with you. Fae magic is much revered among us," said Attania. "Onyx, would you show her the way?"

A black dragon so shiny, Skye could barely see his individual scales, began to move down one of the tunnels that led off the main open cavern. Skye followed him into the darkness.

The tunnel opened up into a fairly small cavern. It was lit by a fire and felt warm to Skye. Two grass green dragons stood over a small yellow hatchling who lay on a bed of dried grass.

"This is Fern and this is Grass, two of our healers. This is Skye, a Fae healer. She has asked if she can be of any help."

"Thank you. If you know what to do, that would be helpful. We have never encountered this type of venom before," said Fern.

Grass bobbed her head in agreement. Onyx turned and walked back down the tunnel, obviously eager to get back to the discussion out front.

"So, if I understand it, one of the wyverns bit this hatchling's tail?"

"Yes," said Grass.

Skye went over to the little one. He was sleeping. She put her hands over him, feeling great heat. There were bite marks on the tail, puncture wounds that went deep. There was little blood and the tail was red, inflamed.

She could feel the poison moving through his veins, slowing everything down. Including his great heart.

"He cannot seem to move anymore," said Fern.

"Do dragons ever use a stimulant?" asked Skye.

"A what?" asked Grass.

"Something to wake you up, make you feel more energetic."

"Yes, sometimes we chew pine bark. Would that help him? I don't think he can chew though."

"I'm not sure yet."

Speeding up his system might just deliver the venom faster. On the other hand, if his heart quit beating, nothing else mattered.

Finally, she said, "I need some fabric. Some chunks of charcoal, and water. I'll make a poultice to put around his tail, see if we can draw some of the venom out. And then we'll need to get some pine bark. Maybe one of you could chew it and put some of the juices into his mouth. Try to get him to swallow it."

Both healers sped from the cave, off to search for what she asked for.

Grass returned first with an old shirt, and a clay pot with chunks of charcoal in it.

"Dylan left this here and forgot to get it," she said of the shirt. "I will fly off and return with some pine bark." And she was gone again.

Skye spread the shirt on the cave floor. Then she took the cold charcoal clumps and set them on the shirt. She looked around and found a chunk of rock to pound the charcoal into a powder. She spread the powder over half of the shirt, then folded the other part of the shirt over the top. When Fern returned with the water, Skye wet the shirt with it. Then she had Fern lift the hatchling's limp tail and wrapped the poultice around it.

"Well, I hope it will help somewhat."

Grass came back with pine bark. Fern had found another clay pot and they both chewed the pine bark and spat into the pot. Skye mixed it with a bit of water to make the liquid runny enough. Then they help the hatchling's mouth open and she dripped some in.

"Swallow, little one," she said.

And he did.

She dripped more in, until the pot was empty. He kept swallowing.

"How much effect would that much pine bark have on you?" Skye asked. "Is it enough for him?"

"It should be more than enough," Fern said.

Skye stood, holding her hands over the hatchling. She felt the venom moving through his blood and pushed it away from his heart. Pushed it towards the tail. For perhaps an hour she worked the venom, forcing it toward the wound, helping it leave the hatchling's body. Until she felt exhausted.

"I think there is nothing more to be done for now. We must wait," said Skye. She sat back on her haunches.

The two healer dragons also sat down. Fern with her nose close to the hatchling's ear. She began to hum an incredibly sweet song to the little one.

Skye hadn't known that dragons sang.

Faerie was a remarkable place with extraordinary creatures.

CHAPTER 37 ~ FIACHNA

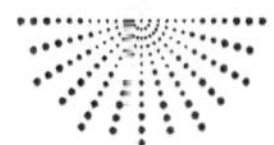

Fiacha could feel the weather warming a bit. Enough to begin melting the snow quickly. Or perhaps this part of Faerie just hadn't received as much snow as where they'd been last.

He walked slowly and silently behind the thickets of bushes and brambles. Careful not to be seen, more careful than usual. Plague had sharper eyes than the original Fomorians. Or maybe he was just more suspicious.

The birds were out this afternoon. Blackcaps and jackdaws making a lot of noise as a golden eagle swooped overhead.

The stone warriors were now east of the dragons' caves. The tallest mountain rose behind them, backed by a series of hills.

Fiachna still sensed the dragons digging deeply inside that mountain. Were they enlarging their caves to fit the new population of hatchlings? Or as a place to dig in defensively, should Fae decide to throw them out of Faerie again? He hoped to never see such a day. It had become clear to him that the dragons were the heart of Faerie. They kept her warm and vibrant. They were an essential part of her.

He and Pearce continued to shadow Balor and his group. They seemed the most dangerous at this point.

The Fomorians had moved down the meadow, in the same

general direction the offspring had gone. Although much more slowly. Obviously not trying to catch up with them.

Fiachna and Pearce stuck to the deep shadows of the woods. Easier now that the snow had melted, their dark figures didn't have to blend into its whiteness. They didn't want to risk Plague spotting them.

Balor hadn't gone far before he stopped to camp again. He ordered his group about, making them build a huge fire and go off to hunt.

Plague he didn't order around. He gave him a seat of honor and set about making him welcome.

The old giant wasn't completely stupid. Fiachna guessed he was trying to make Plague feel welcome. Win him over, so he'd divulge the offsprings' plans.

It was nearly dark before Elatha and Conand returned, dragging some poor farmer's cow. They tossed the dead beast onto the blazing fire.

The smoke drifted over to Fiachna and Pearce. Bringing with it the scent of roasting meat. Fiachna's stomach growled in response.

Fiachna took the first watch, while Pearce rested. At least they had blankets to wrap themselves in.

He watched the Fomorians eat and argue. All except Balor who sat talking quietly to Plague. Eventually Balor stood, stretched and walked off into the bushes as if to piss. He had his back to the others and they probably couldn't see him behind a hedgerow. But Fiachna could. In the light of the full moon.

He watched Balor remove the kerchiefs and gaze at the bushes surrounding him with his baleful eye. Nothing happened. No bushes flashing into flames. Fiachna was willing to bet they weren't even withered.

Balor's eye seemed damaged enough as to be non-functional. At least temporarily. Giants were as strong as Fae. He might heal completely, but at least for now, one of his weapons didn't work. Which made him less cocky but more dangerous.

Balor quietly put his kerchiefs back on and returned to the fire. Fiachna didn't see him speak again for the rest of the time he watched the giant.

About halfway through the night, Fiachna woke Pearce and curled up in the blanket. He slept soundly. Near dawn, he was woken by almost silent footsteps. The other stone warriors had caught up with them. They carried two haunches of deer, one for Pearce and one for Fiachna.

Alain said the others didn't need any more to eat, having stuffed themselves before sleeping by the fire. Fiachna chewed the dried out cold meat, savoring the smokiness. It wasn't the best he'd ever had, but he relished every bite he took. Only eating a few mouthfuls, he went back to sleep until roused by one of the others. The Fomorians were on the move again.

Fiachna wrapped the meat in his blanket and tied it over one shoulder like a sling, so it was out of his way. The dark gray clouds threatened rain. Making everything look so dark, it was if the sun had never risen.

They followed the Fomorians farther down the meadow. Elatha was tracking something. Probably the offspring. Balor's group went right up to the barrier. Led by Plague.

Who then walked through the barrier. Balor followed him, as did all the others.

The Fomorians were in Faerie!

Fiachna's mouth dropped open as he and Pearce looked at each other. They had no idea how it had been managed.

The stone warriors stopped in their track and became invisible. The Fomorians passed around the thickets which hid the Fae, and began to move deeper into Faerie following the trail of the offspring.

"What happened during your watch?" Fiachna asked Pearce.

"Not much. More eating. The usual arguing and fighting." He turned to Orrell. "And during yours?"

"More of the same. Except they stood in a circle and each pierced their thumb with a knife. Then the big black one, Plague you call him, he went around the inside of the circle and pressed his thumb against everyone else's. Sort of like a ritual maybe. Becoming one of their group. That is what I thought. Then they went to sleep," said Orrell.

Fiachna said, "They shared blood. He gave the Fomorians some of his Fae blood. So they could pass through the boundary."

Pearce said, "We need to warn the palace."

Fiachna tried to send, but the palace was too far away.

"Alain, you are the strongest sender. Do you know where the palace is?"

Alain pointed.

"Yes. I want you to hurry towards it. Staying away from any Fomorians and remaining unseen by them. They are heading away from it, for now. Send to Alana, or other Council elders, often. Until you reach them. Orrell you go with him. If you pass through any villages, warn them, but do not tarry. We must warn the Council so they can act."

Alain nodded and he and Orrell were gone.

Fiachna hoped that the Council had come up with a plan by now. Because he had none. He motioned to the others and they went back to shadowing the Fomorians, keeping a look out for the offspring.

CHAPTER 38 ~ EGAN

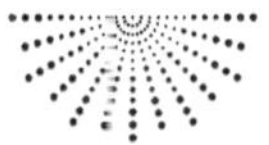

EGAN HAD SPENT THE LAST TWO DAYS RIDING DIFFERENT dragons from the palace and passing over various villages. With no success. Spike carried him this time. The dragon had been out flying the other days when Egan had been ready to go.

It was now the end of the third day. They were circling over an area east of the dragon caves. Egan had walked all over this area.

As he looked down from Spike's back, the village was visible beneath him. It had a large limestone structure that functioned as a wall and which hid it when approaching from the direction of the palace. If one was coming from outside Faerie, the trees hid the limestone structure. Egan had never noticed the limestone wall when he'd been to the village the first time with Skye, Adaire, Pearce and Glenna.

He had Spike put him down in a clearing outside the village, on the far side. The village was fully hidden by the forest. The Fae who lived here must be very secretive. The buildings looked ancient. Had the village been built before Faerie was closed the first time? From the days when Fae needed to hide from humans?

"What will you do if she is not here?" asked Spike.

"I don't know. Return to the palace perhaps."

"Should I wait?"

"No. If this isn't it I'll walk."

"Then farewell, and good luck," said Spike. Then the black dragon flew off. Egan thought Spike looked a bit dejected.

He took a deep breath, reaching down into himself and bringing his energy up a couple of notches. Prepared for anything.

The surrounding woods were a mixture of yew and some sort of deciduous tree with grayish bark. The gray barked ones grew close together and in places the forest had become a thicket of branches.

He followed a trail which crossed a stream narrow enough for him to jump over. He took a sip of it and the water tasted fresh and clean. It quenched his thirst and he enjoyed it despite the coldness.

He surprised a brown rabbit who disappeared into the woodland. Unlike many places in Faerie, this one wasn't highly cultivated. There were downed logs for Fae to hide behind and thickets of plants, which in other places, would have been thinned by earth spirits. Perhaps there weren't many earth spirits in this village.

He felt nervous. What if she told him to go away? Should he stick around and show her he could be counted on? Or respect her wishes and go away?

Egan kept walking. He could smell smoke. He hoped it was her, roasting peppers.mHis mouth watered at the thought. Her peppers had been extraordinary.

The village was suddenly in front of him as the forest opened up. Wooden buildings sat beneath the high tree canopy. Close to a blazing fire, a wizened old fire Fae was pulling clay pots out of ashes. Egan knew she had been firing them with a fire built in a hole in the ground. She examined each one and held it into a flame to burn off any debris, then set it close to the edge of the flames, so the pot wouldn't cool too quickly and crack.

Her skin was entirely covered with black scales, an ancient elder. She looked at him, recognizing distant kin and nodded her head. He returned the nod.

She returned to her work. The pots she was pulling out were glazed in intricate designs in dark colors. She was truly a superb artist. If he hadn't been searching for Lassair it would have been pleasant to sit and pass the time with this elder. She was far more powerful than Conley, but probably not interested in such things as the Council.

Egan continued walking through the village. He passed an earth Fae sitting on a rustic wooden chair weaving strands of soft looking creamy brown wool. Possibly from bilberry goats. There were several herds which roamed through Faerie.

Farther down through the center of the village, two Fae worked on carving designs into a door frame. At their feet lay piles of pale wood shavings, probably used by the potter to fire her pots. They waved at him as he passed and Egan waved back.

The next house had a table out front with glass bottles. They were filled with liquid and the tops wrapped with leather. Egan guessed they were mead. Most of the grape vines grew farther south where it was a bit warmer.

Next there was a small fire, surrounded by rocks larger than someone's head. On top of which lay a metal grate covered with peppers, roasting in the flames.

The smell was extraordinary.

He looked around, but saw no one. The tiny stone cottage looked empty. The door was open and he peered in, but it seemed empty. Although he smelled Lassair. He would recognize her sultry, smoky fragrance anywhere.

He sat down on a stone bench in front of the cottage. The sun cut through the trees, lighting up the bench and warming him.

He had no intention of moving until she told him to.

CHAPTER 39 ~ SPIKE

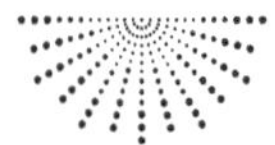

Spike returned home. It was time for the evening meal for those who wanted it. He wasn't hungry so soon after eating yesterday. He could try to sneak past the wyverns and go listen to the wise ones.

At some point he had to end this. He had to stop avoiding them and live his life again. Perhaps today was the day he could help them understand.

The outside cave area was packed with dragons. It wasn't dinnertime, it was a weir meeting. He landed in the only space available and clumsily bumped into Iru, who snarled at him.

"Sorry," said Spike.

"This is all your fault," Iru said, loudly.

"What?" asked Spike.

"You brought those wyverns here!" Iru bellowed.

What had they done? The crowd parted and he was shoved to the front, protesting. Attania stood in front of the painted wall, her forehead wrinkled with irritation.

"Are you finished, Iru?"

"It is his fault," said a reddish brown dragon who Spike had never liked. Apparently the feeling was returned.

Attania asked, "Would you like to defend yourself?"

Spike gave a deep sigh and took the speaker's position.

"I do not know what has happened here. But I do know that when I came upon a hatchling at the palace, lost, tired, cold and hungry, I brought her here. And when she had recovered, we searched for her weir. There were four more hatchlings there. Starving and cold. With no adults to be found. I did what I thought was the right thing to do. I brought them here where they could be fed and cared for. It is what we dragons do. That which we think is right. To do less would make us less than dragons."

Attania thumped her tail in applause. As did most of the crowd. As did the fuchsia dragon. He stared at her, his eyes widening.

"Spike did what he should have done. He did not know what we know now. He is not at fault for today's happenings. And neither is Ragwort. They are not manageable by only one dragon. We need at least four caretakers. Four strong dragons who they respect."

"They respect Spike," said Ragwort.

"I am not a good caretaker," said Spike.

"They do not need a good caretaker," yelled a dragon in the crowd. "They need to be taught to hunt."

Spike said, "No one dragon could do that alone. They are too rambunctious to keep track of."

"I will help," said the fuchsia dragon.

Attania said, "Thank you Valerian. We will find someone to look after your other charges. Ragwort, I think that is you. All right, we need two more dragons. Spike and Valerian need to sleep. If someone does not speak up, then I will choose two of you."

Valerian, her name was Valerian. Spike was willing to suffer being around the wyverns if he could be around her also. He felt his scales flush red with passion, beneath the black. He knew no one else could see it though.

No one else volunteered. Attania, finally exasperated, named

Carbon and Keirosum. Two good choices. Both were strong enough to not be afraid of the wyverns, but honest enough to do their best.

The four of them spoke and decided Carbon and Keirosum would spend the night with the wyverns, after they ate. So Valerian and Spike would go speak with the hatchlings now and let them know what was happening.

Valerian led the way to the cave where the wyverns were being held. Like prisoners, Spike noted. The open door was covered with iron mesh held up by rocks. Maximus was on the opposite side of the mesh, making sure they couldn't knock it down.

The wyverns were all curled up together, but got up when the mesh was pushed aside. Maximus left.

"How are all of you?" asked Spike.

"Scared," said Bluefire.

"This is Valerian. She and I will be your daytime caretakers from now on."

"No more Ragweed?" asked Pine.

"No more Ragweed," said Valerian.

"Who takes care of us at night?" asked Yew.

"Carbon and Keirosum."

The wyverns looked at each other, but no one seemed to recognize the names.

"We will have some rules here," said Spike. "I do not know what Ragweed expected of you."

"To behave," sniped Birch.

"Did he say why?" asked Valerian.

"No," said Birch.

Spike said, "I do not know what wyverns normally do, but dragons live close together in a small area. As adults we must treat each other with kindness and respect. I expect that of you."

Valerian said, "Our young are hatched without the knowledge of adults. They learn as they grow. That is why our hatchlings tumble and bite and are mean to each other. So they can learn to hunt and fight. You wyverns are different. It seems that you are hatched knowing things. You know how to fly, you didn't have to be taught. I am guessing that you probably know how to hunt. We will find out. If you do not, then we will teach you."

Spike said, "Because you already know things, we must treat you like almost adults. And because your bite contains poison one rule that is unbreakable is that there will be no biting."

He looked at Hawthorn who had been completely silent the entire time.

"I am in trouble," she said.

"Did you bite the hatchling?"

"He said mean things. Said I was not a real dragon because I only had two legs."

"Are you a real dragon?" Spike asked.

"I do not know. Am I?"

"Yes," said Valerian. "We are all different. You are even more different, having only two legs, but you are most certainly a real dragon. And being a real dragon means you did not have to let his teasing bother you. Right?"

"I guess," said Hawthorn.

"We must find ways for all of you to deal with your anger. There will always be someone trying to light you up like a fire. To let them do so gives them power over you," said Spike

"I see," said Hawthorn. "That is very wise. I will remember that."

"Me too," said Yew.

"All of us will," said Bluefire.

Pine and Birch nodded.

"Have you eaten yet?" asked Valerian.

"Yes," said Pine.

"Well then, Carbon and Keirosum will be here after they've eaten. Suppose you all curl up and I will tell you a story of great dragons who lived a very long time ago," said Valerian.

"No one has ever told us a story," said Bluefire.

"Well, it is about time, then is it not?" asked Spike.

He lay down and curled up with them while Valerian began the story.

"Long ago when Faerie was young and the world was new, dragons lived much as they do now. They painted caves, hunted deer and salmon, lived and loved. Then humans came to this part of the world. At first the humans left dragons alone. Most of them lived in Faerie anyway and humans, being superstitious, didn't often stray into Faerie. There were a few solitary dragons who lived alone in small caves. They didn't seem to need other dragons much and spent their time pondering the mysteries of the stars above and the inner workings of our earth."

"Abdele the green, was one such dragon. Although she was a wyvern, as a young dragon, she questioned everything. When she grew to adulthood, Abdele left Faerie to wander the world. To find out what humans thought, and did, and how they lived. Far across the sea, she loved a human for that one's entire life, from childhood to doddering steps until death. The villagers found her with the dead human and got the wrong idea, as humans often do. They thought she killed the human and chased her away.

"Abdele was drowning in grief at her human's death and retreated to a cave in the nearby mountains. But humans had discovered dragons existed. They saw dragons as a threat and used their religion to justify the death of any dragon. Humans began to hunt dragons."

Spike watched the wyvern's eyes. They were completely mesmerized by Valerian's story.

"Now, a human on horseback with a spear is not usually a threat to a dragon, but Abdele was heartbroken. She hadn't eaten in months. Only drank the trickles of rain falling from the sky. She was doing poorly when last another dragon went to visit her, encouraging to return to Faerie.

"Abdele told him great stories about humans and their world.

She had much wisdom to share, but she refused to return to Faerie. He left, carrying her wisdom to Faerie.

"Several days later, a man came to her cave. He tried to lance her with his spear. She spat venom at him, most likely having been surprised and shaken out of sleep. The man avoided the venom, but his armor cracked into several pieces. He ran forward and pierced her with his sword. Destroying her already broken heart.

We only know what happened from the stories he told, bragging about killing a dragon. We never found her body, just pieces of it, after the humans chopped it up. We still mourn for Abdele the tender-hearted. Killed by a monster."

CHAPTER 40 ~ SOLANGE

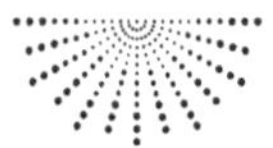

SOLANGE WOKE THE MORNING AFTER YULE WHEN THE SUN blasted through the window. She was back in her own room. Dylan's room. He lay beside her sleeping. Dylan's side of the bed was damp from his sprite body leaking water.

She didn't mind. It felt wonderful to sleep with him again.

He was deeply asleep, his eyelids twitching. Dreaming. It was as if the past several weeks hadn't happened. Her sickness and their separation.

Except that the pall of depression that had hung over him seemed gone. He was smiling, even in his sleep.

Solange rolled over onto her back and sighed. Last night had been glorious.

She glanced up at the ceiling and then looked again. Stunned.

A framed canvas was attached to the ceiling, over the bed. A huge painting, one of Dylan's fabulous underwater scenes. Water Fae floated just beneath the surface, fish swam past. Frogs and salamanders clung to water plants. In the air above the water, dragonflies lurked in the shadows. She could study it forever and still see new things.

He'd said he had a surprise for her. That he'd show it to her in the morning. She hadn't expected this.

So he had been listening to her complain through the door. About every little thing and he'd set to work, changing what he could.

She smiled, rolled back over and kissed his cheek.

"Thank you."

"For what?" he mumbled.

"For the surprise."

His eyes opened and he looked up and then at her.

"I had to do something to pass the time when you were sick."

"I'm glad you found something. Now get up sleepyhead. You might not need to eat, but I want breakfast before we leave."

"Leave for where?" he looked confused.

"Dragon caves."

"Oh, that." He sat up, rubbing his eyes.

She got out of bed, washed her face and dressed in warm clothes. Most Fae would be dressing down below in the entryway, but since she was always cold, Solange kept a stash of winter clothes up in the room. She was only comfortable with going naked in the heat of the summer.

Dylan ran his hands through his hair and waited for her.

They kissed, again, and went downstairs.

Dylan headed over to the collection of clothes to find something to wear outside.

Solange went into the throne room, finding it crowded with Fae who were going to the caves and others just there for an early breakfast. There were also a few Fae sleeping on benches who had obviously not left after the Yule celebration ended last night. Or maybe early this morning.

Solange grabbed a scone, sausages and eggs, and poured a cup of black tea.

She really did have to remember to speak to the kitchen about getting hold of some chocolate.

Meredith was sitting alone and sipping a cup of tea. Solange sat next to her.

"So, how are you enjoying your freedom?" Meredith asked.

"I am so relieved not to be trapped in that room anymore."

"Apparently, so is Skye. She's vanished."

Solange was shocked. "That's right, I didn't see her last night. I know she was dying to go out flying. Are you worried?"

"Not yet. Perhaps she went to stay with the other sylphs."

"Well, I'm sure she'll turn up," said Solange. "Are you coming today?"

"Yes, I believe I will. I should probably go get dressed. But I'm feeling particularly lazy after last night."

"That was quite a party you threw."

"Yes, it was. Just wait till you see what we've got planned for the next one."

"Really, you've planned Imbolc already?"

"Actually, I was thinking of Beltane."

A thundering noise announced the arrival of the dragons.

"Okay, I'm off," said Meredith, rising from the bench and setting her mug on a cart.

"See you in a few," said Solange, gulping down the last of her eggs. She finished the lovely sausages, washed them down with the strong black tea, then took her dishes to the cart. She took the scone off the plate and stashed it in the pocket of her coat. She wasn't about to give it up.

Dylan was in the hallway, pulling on a light jacket made of sealskin. Which would repel his water. He wore nothing else, insisting the jacket was enough.

She took his arm and they went out the door. Ethelgarde had been the first to arrive. He wore a rigging which would carry at least ten Fae. She and Dylan were among the first outside, so they climbed up, followed by Meredith.

After they'd tied themselves in, Solange sat back and savored the scone. A buttery, biscuity pastry peppered with dried blueberries and cardamon. Whose flavor sort of unraveled in her mouth. It tasted wonderful. The kitchen Fae made the most extraordinary food. Which always left her feeling like she was eating a work of art.

Other Fae climbed up and by the time Solange finished the scone, Ethelgarde was ready to take off. He ran off the edge of the courtyard and the stairs dropped away as his great wings flapped up and down. He curved, gliding around the empty space, flapping his wings until they had risen over the tops of the trees. Then he flew towards the mountain.

The cool air lashed her face, even though she knew Ethelgarde was flying slowly. Her hair whipped around her. She'd forgotten to tie it back. It had been a while since she'd ridden a dragon.

About halfway there, Meredith, who was sitting just behind her gasped.

Dylan asked, "What is it?"

"Fomorians. Inside Faerie. One of the stone warriors is sending to the Council. He's too far from the palace to reach everyone."

Dylan looked worried. "Tell Ethelgarde to tell the dragons who are still at the palace. They can let the others know. Dragons can send farther than Fae." Then as if he realized Meredith had probably never spoken to a dragon before, he said, "I'll do it."

He fell silent. Solange knew Dylan was speaking with the dragon. How had Fomorians gotten through the boundary?

Dylan asked, "Where are the Fomorians?"

"Somewhere west of us, I think. They were traveling from about the center of the northern boundary."

"So we might fly right over them."

"Yes. We might."

Not that there's anything we can do about it. There was still no plan to deal with them. Solange felt guilty she hadn't been able to help. Even though she'd been sick.

"I should return to the palace," said Meredith.

"The last dragon has just taken off. We're closer to the Fomorians at the dragon caves. Most of the elders will be there."

"Except Alana and Brian."

"But they know where we are. We can send another dragon back for them," said Dylan.

"That's a good idea. Please do. I will send to those Council members I can reach."

Dylan went silent again, making the request. Solange tried to see below, but the dragon's great bulk and his wings blocked most of her view. She didn't know what to do about the Fomorians, but she did know that all hell was about to break loose.

CHAPTER 41 ~ LEA

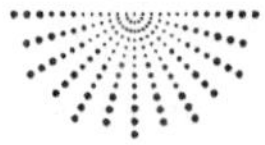

LEA WAS RIDING A GREEN DRAGON NAMED GOSHANIA. SHE SAT between Ogden and Aura. Aura was particularly excited. Even though the sylph said she could easily have flown the distance herself.

Riding a dragon was such fun. Lea felt thrilled when Goshania ran off the edge of the courtyard, flapping those magnificent wings. Creating a wind like Lea had rarely felt. She was relieved to be strapped on so tightly, and relieved that Willow had insisted she wear so many clothes. The fur gloves felt especially nice on her beaten skin.

She loved seeing the land from so high above. One could see what Faerie really was. A puzzle of forests, meadows, clearings and grasslands. Separated by a few streams, rivers and lakes. It was a glorious place.

At the same time, Aura sucked in her breath and Ogden gasped. Lea could feel the shock and fear wrenching them.

"What is wrong?" she asked.

"Fomorians. Inside Faerie," said Ogden

Lea's heart sank.

"What can I do to help?" she asked.

"Stay calm and if you can quickly come up with a way to

defeat the Fomorians, then please tell us. We have been searching for a solution for a very long time," said Aura.

She had no solution.

"Have all of the elders tried to confront them at once?"

"No. When they were first imprisoned in the vault, Meredith was the only elder there. Although she did draw on all the energy of the Fae who were near. Some of them elders," said Aura."

"And when we tricked them into leaving Faerie and putting the boundary up again, there were elders involved. But never all at once, focused on one spell."

"Do we have anything to lose. By confronting them with all of us?"

"Just our lives," said Ogden.

"But if they are already in Faerie destroying things, as is their way, then they will attempt to kill us one by one, perhaps succeeding. Am I correct?" asked Lea.

"Yes," said Ogden. "Balor's desire is to kill all of us and destroy Faerie."

"Perhaps we can attack them. All of us together. I do not have masses of power, but I have gathered a fair amount having simply been alive for such a long time."

"The Fomorians have lived for longer," said Aura.

"Yes, but their magic is very different than ours," said Ogden.

"What shall we do to them?" asked Lea.

"Kill them," said Ogden.

"Has that ever worked?" asked Lea. "Trying to kill an immortal being? Better to put them to sleep for a very long time and try to find a way to disable them forever."

"We tried that with the vault," said Aura.

"That was not long enough," said Lea. "We need to put them asleep for thousands upon thousands of years. It might take that long for us to come up with a way to finally defeat them."

Ogden said, "All right, that is one possible idea. We need several. We will meet at the dragons' caves and decide there. It would be good to have more than one plan to choose from."

"Perhaps the dragons can help us craft a plan," said Lea. "Have they ever been involved in the Council before?"

Aura said, "No. They have not. Not in our lifetime at least. They lived in Faerie in ancient times. It is possible they may have been involved in the distant past. We have consulted them about the war, but never invited their participation on the Council."

"Perhaps, it is time. I know of one elder, Silver, who is remarkable. She may have ideas that we cannot see."

"I think you have a good idea there. Dragon magic is so unlike our own. They may be able to come up with something that we cannot think of."

They continued to come up with possible plans for the remainder of the ride to the dragons' caves. Which went far too quickly. Lea felt surprise when the mountain came into view.

CHAPTER 42 ~ SKYE

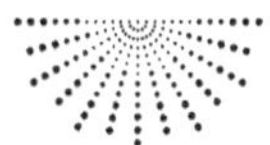

SKYE, GRASS AND FERN STAYED WITH THE INJURED hatchling all night. Skye had spent so much of the last few weeks sleeping that she felt no more need to do so. She periodically checked his breathing. His heart seemed to have picked up.

When dawn came and Skye heard other dragons stirring in the main cavern, she had Fern get some more charcoal and water. Skye removed the poultice and emptied it out in the fire. The wet charcoal sizzled.

The hatchling's tail look slightly less red, a little less inflamed. She cleaned the wound again with leftover water from the previous night. Then she rinsed the shirt in the fresh water Fern brought and began again. Crushing the charcoal, wrapping it up in the shirt, then Grass lifted the hatchling's tail up so Skye could wrap the new poultice around it.

She did more energy work on him, trying to help his body fight the toxins. Skye could sense the complexity of the wyvern's venom. When she returned to the palace, she would try to concoct a healing potion for the dragons. It would take some time.

"How do dragons normally cleanse the inside of your bodies?

Fae and humans drink water or eat food that contains a lot of water, like green plants, to flush poisons out of our bodies."

"We rarely encounter poisons," said Grass.

"Most of our water comes from the blood and juices of creatures we kill and cook."

"What meat is the juiciest?"

"They are all alike," said Fern. "It is how much they are roasted that is important."

"So, uncooked meat has more blood?"

Fern bobbed her head in acknowledgement.

"Can you clean this and fill it up with blood?" Skye asked, holding out one of the clay pots.

"Yes," said Fern, taking the pot and leaving.

While she was gone, the hatchling began to whimper.

"It is okay, little one," said Skye. "You just keep being strong. Keep that heart beating."

Grass began to stroke his shoulders and ribs.

Fern returned fairly quickly and they woke him up and put some blood in his mouth, he swallowed, hungrily. They were able to get the entire pot down him, then let him return to sleep.

Skye hoped that they had done the right thing. That this would remove the toxins from his body. She wanted him to grow up to be a healthy, courageous dragon.

Skye felt suddenly tired. She had to pace herself and not get over tired. She hadn't been well that long. She curled up next to the hatchling, sharing his bed of dried grass and fell fast asleep.

When she woke it was to a commotion at the end of the tunnel. Grass and Fern were looking that direction.

"What's happening?" asked Skye, sitting up.

"Fae are here. To see the hatchlings, but something is wrong," said Grass.

"Will you go find out what it is? I'll check on this one."

Grass ran down the hallway.

Skye crouched over the hatchling. His little heart was

beating faster, his entire body had what felt like a better energy to it. She'd change out the poultice again this evening.

"I think he's a little better," said Skye. "Just a little."

Grass came running back.

"There are Fomorians in Faerie!"

Skye drooped a bit then.

"I'd better go out front. I'll be back when I can. If I'm not here at dinnertime, then can you remove the shirt, clean it and the wound with fresh clean water, break up more cold charcoal and wrap his tail up again? And feed him more blood tonight?"

"Yes," said Fern. "I was watching. I can take over now."

"Good. You two should take turns resting and eating. Take care of yourselves as well."

"Thank you very much for your help," said Grass.

"We would not have thought to try any of this. We must speak more about Fae healing," said Fern.

"Yes," said Skye. "I believe we have much to teach each other. I must go now."

With that, she walked to the front of the cave to see what she could do out there. Fomorians. How had they gotten in? She went up to Meredith and Aura, who stood looking worried. And sad.

"Skye!" said Meredith. "I was worried about you, when you didn't come back last night. What's wrong, you're all black?"

Skye looked at her black hands and realized she'd smeared charcoal everywhere. She held up her hands.

"Charcoal. I've been helping an injured dragon. So, I heard the bad news. Where are they?"

"Just inside the border, not far east of here," said Meredith.

"Why around here? Are they coming to attack the dragons? That makes no sense."

"We're not sure. We suspect that's just where they entered," Meredith said.

"How, how did they get in?"

"They shared blood with one of the offspring, Plague. For some reason, the boundary now recognizes them as Fae instead of repelling them. The other offspring are also here, but at odds with Balor's band. It is too late to change the spell on the boundary, which is very complex and would take the work of several skilled Fae to unweave and reweave again. But I suppose we must try."

Skye shuddered.

"That might mean they're also carrying whatever he gave me."

Aura put her hand over her mouth, "Oh."

"That is possible. I don't know," said Meredith.

"What are you going to do?" asked Skye.

"The Council is gathering. We're waiting for a dragon to bring Brian and Alana. They hadn't planned on coming today."

"But we have several very good ideas," said Aura. "We will come up with something. We have no choice. Letting the Fomorians have Faerie is not an option."

"That sounds like something Meredith would say," said Skye.

"See, we are even beginning to talk alike," said Aura.

Conley came over to join them, burning more brightly than she'd ever seen him. Skye moved away to let the Council begin their work. She walked over to one of the fires and just stood there, eyes glazed. In shock. Even she knew that.

"Can I get you a piece of meat?" asked a warm voice she hadn't heard for a long time.

"Aidan."

"Hello Skye," he held out his arms and she hugged him. She had missed him so. Tears began to trickle down her face.

"Hey, hey, you'll mar that beautiful charcoal colored face. What's wrong?"

"Formorians."

"I know. They're becoming a real pain in the arse. I think we should take care of them once and for all, don't you?"

He was teasing her.

"How?"

"I don't know. But the elders will come up with something. I know they will. We can't give up. We can't let them have Faerie. I know you believe that too."

"When I came back, I looked for you."

"I've been out in the southwest edge of Faerie. For what seems like forever. Just guarding the boundaries. And trying to help heal some of the fire Fae. They're all so depleted. I came here just a bit ago and Ethelgarde told me that Egan spent time in the cook fires here, and got blasted occasionally by dragon fire. It healed and strengthened him. So I stepped in for just a few minutes. It was amazing. I think we've found the ultimate way to heal fire Fae. I can't wait to tell them all."

"You do look healthy. Better than I've ever seen you," said Skye. That must be why Conley looked so rejuvenated too.

"Anyway, maybe we can end this nasty war once and for all. Then you and I can be together again. I have missed you so much," he squeezed her again.

"I've missed you too. You know that if the war ends, I need to go back to Glastonbury."

"I'd follow you there. Even if it meant I'd need to hide in a human body again, just so I wouldn't scare the locals. I mean, I'm not going to get any more presentable to them, am I?"

He was right. Fire Fae only got more scaled as they acquired more power and age. And he had gained more scales in just the last half a year since she'd seen him.

"I'd like it if you came with me. Someday, we might not have to hide."

"I would do it though. Just to be with you." He held her for what seemed like a very long time.

Then Aidan said, "I really should gather with all the other fire Fae and return to the fire. We need to get as strong as we can. I believe Faerie is going to need all our strength and courage today."

She nodded and kissed him deeply, feeling the flames of his passion.

Then she turned and walked away. Finding the courage and strength to consider what the air spirits should be doing to prepare.

CHAPTER 43 ~ FIACHNA

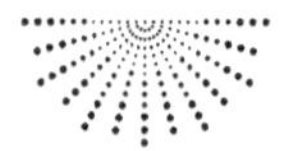

Fiachna and the other warriors stood on an outcropping of standing stones that topped the hill, blending into the uprights. In the valley down below them Balor's band of Fomorians faced the offspring.

The valley was surrounded by woodlands on two sides and mountainous slopes in front of Fiachna and to his right. The offspring were more numerous, but they were looking for a way out. They didn't look like they wanted to fight. The ones in the back kept turning their heads, this way and that, searching for the best escape route.

Or perhaps, they were expecting to be attacked.

Alain and Orrell came up from behind Fiachna and blended in with the stones.

Alain sent, *"I contacted the Council. Most of them are at the dragon caves and they expect the others soon. They said to stay near the Fomorians and be ready for anything. But not too near."*

Fiachna looked at Alain, who grinned.

"Do they have a plan?"

"I was under the impression that they do not. But they will soon."

Fiachna nodded and relayed the information to his warriors. They waited quite a while.

Balor paced back and forth in front of his group. Which still included Plague. Fiachna was not certain whose side Plague was on. He might be a plant. His exchange of blood may have been to give the Fomorians the disease he carried. The one that infected Skye. Or perhaps he really had just given them his blood to get them into Faerie. But why? Why did he differ so much from the other offspring? Fiachna would find out the answer when the Fomorians started fighting each other, but first came the build up.

Balor beat his chest and roared insults about the offspring. Their weaknesses and their cowardice. The offspring still looked like they didn't want to fight.

In the bright daylight Fiachna noticed that there was a dark stain on Balor's kerchief. Right in the center of the forehead. Had Balor tested out his eye again in the time since Fiachna had seen him try it? Did the eye work, or was it permanently damaged?

Fiachna glanced off to the right. He could see the dragons' mountain rising up behind the foothills.

There had been a lot of dragons flying back and forth this morning. Had Balor seen them? Was he worried about them?

From up here on the hill, Fiachna had a spectacular view of the battlefield. It would be best to wait and see how this played out. See if the Fomorians wiped each other out. Was that even possible.? Or at least let them exhaust each other. If any of Balor's group ran, they might come back up where he and the stone warriors stood. Most likely they'd flee into the woods to Fiachna's left. That would be less effort and better cover. The he received a message from Meredith.

"Fiachna, can you hear me?"

"Yes."

"We're at the dragons' caves. Where are you?"

"At the foot of the mountains. We are blending in with the standing stones, do you remember the ones for old Dunstan? We are above the Fomorians and their offspring. They are preparing to fight each other."

"Are they now? Well, that's just lovely. We're gathering here. The dragons and the fire Fae. The sylphs have been called. And the earth spirits, too. Let us know when to move."

"I think we should wait until after they pummel each other. Wear them down a bit, but I think they might run into the woods on the east and north sides of this valley, if they decide to escape. We should be prepared for that."

"I'll see what I can do."

"Meredith, Domnu's not here."

"I believe she got tired of Balor's quest for vengeance and has gone back to care for the sea. At least that's what it feels like to me."

"But if we kill all her kin then she might seek revenge. We should be prepared."

"You're right of course. I don't see that we have a choice here."

"No. We don't. We'll let you know what is happening. Right now Balor is just posturing, baiting the offspring."

"Okay, I'll see what I can do to shore up those woods to catch any stragglers."

Fiachna continued waiting and watching. Sizing up the Fomorians and their offspring. Trying to figure out who would run and who would fight.

Trying to stay in the present and pull the power of the stones beneath his feet up into himself. He knew the other stone Fae did the same. It was as it always had been.

The stones were the bones of the earth and the stone Fae were the defenders of Faerie.

CHAPTER 44 ~ EGAN

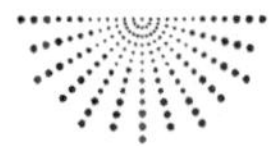

EGAN WAS STARTLED OUT OF DOZING WHEN HE FELT A SHADOW fall across him. He opened his eyes and looked up to see Lassair standing in front of him, hands on her hips. At her feet was a bundle of dried sticks. Firewood.

The look on her face said she wasn't happy to see him.

"Hello," he said, looking around for Aine. He saw her down the road, talking to the elder fire Fae.

"Why are you here?"

"I came to see you."

"It took you this long?"

"This village isn't an easy place to find, but yes. It took me this long. I have been rather distracted. Then after that, too proud. Then too stupid."

"Well, at least you know yourself."

There was an awkward silence.

He'd forgotten how amazingly strong she was. That's what had drawn him to her in the first place.

Then he felt a call so strong it blasted through everything. Lassair also had a shocked look on her face.

"Fire Fae! All who can hear me, I am Conley of the old fires. Lend me

your energy. All who are close enough come. To the Standing Stones of Old Dunstan. Be wary and stay hidden. Fomorians have entered Faerie. We must destroy them."

"Is that near here?" asked Egan.

"Just through the forest," she yelled back at him and raced down the road towards Aine.

He followed her. The two earth Fae had stopped carving the house and were listening intently. So was the Fae who had been weaving and an earth Fae who stood by the bottles of mead. They were being called too.

"Lassair, you stay here with Aine. I am stronger that you," said the elder fire Fae.

"No Magda, you cannot walk well enough."

"I can stay by myself," said Aine, hands on her hips, just like her mother, Aidan noticed.

The Fae who had been weaving and the mead maker came over and said, "We have little power and never have. We will take Aine in the other direction and go hide in the woods. In a tree hollow. They will not find us. Now go. Save Faerie for all of us."

That seemed to be an agreeable solution to both Aine and the elder fire Fae. They nodded and began heading down the road through town, following the two earth Fae who had been carving wood.

"Is this the fastest way?" asked Egan.

Lassair glared at him.

He shut up and followed them, giving his arm to Magda, the elder, helping aid her physical strength.

After a time, they left the road and followed the earth Fae through the woods. It was a narrow deer trail and tree branches continually slapped him across the face. The trail was narrow but not tall. Perhaps not deer after all. Were there still fauns in these woods? That was an enchanting thought.

The elder was behind him and she was tiring. He stopped and bent over.

Egan whispered, "Climb on my back. I will carry you."

Magda wasn't too proud to decline. After she'd crawled up, he hooked his arms around her thighs. She weighed next to nothing, but she was running so much heat and power that he nearly stumbled from the sensation?

"Are you all right?" Magda whispered.

"You are so powerful," he whispered.

She giggled almost silently. As they got closer to the Fomorians, Egan could hear Balor yelling. There was a stony area in the forest, just a ways in.

The five of them crouched, just behind the massive chunk of limestone. Egan held on to its weathered surface, feeling the fractures of the giant piece of rock which extended far back below their feet.

They could see a bit of what was happening in the large grassy clearing. Balor was close enough to that Egan could smell his stench.

Egan used his power to mask all of them, fire and earth Fae. To make them invisible and to hide their power.

Magda sent to him, *"Thank you."*

He nodded.

Far up on the hill behind the Fomorians stood the standing stones Conley had described. Egan sensed Fae up there. They would be stone warriors, invisible to any except one who had traveled with them and knew their habits.

Egan sent, *"Fiachna? Pierce? I am down in the forest below you. If you need me."*

"You saw us?" sent Fiachna.

"No. Just a lucky guess."

"We will call if we need you."

Egan sensed the shimmering presence of other Fae filling the woods behind them and behind the Fomorian offspring, but he couldn't see any of them. Nor could he read their power. They were masking it, just as he was.

He had difficulty seeing the Fomorian offspring through the

trees and shrubbery. Unable to count them and figure out exactly which ones were present. He was closer to Balor's group and could count them. How clever were the offspring? Did their Fae blood allow them to mask themselves?

He waited.

CHAPTER 45 ~ SPIKE

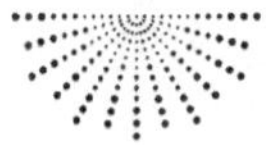

Spike followed the wyverns through the forest and they trailed Valerian.

He smiled. They were clearly as enraptured of her as he was. She'd completely won them over with the story last night.

Now they were out hunting. The young wyverns had really taken to it. They'd brought down a hare and devoured it. It hadn't been much divided between the five of them, but they had loved the fresh, raw meat.

The wise ones, the dragon elders, had been told by Fae that wyverns rarely carried fire. So if they couldn't breathe fire, then perhaps they would be better eating raw meat.

Valerian was searching for something a bit larger than a hare. She stopped at the edge of the woods and huddled the wyverns all around her.

Valerian whispered to them, "In these woods six deer are hiding. We ever only take one from a herd. If there's one injured or old and slow, we take it first. Allowing the healthy deer to thrive and have babies. So that in the future we will continue to have food. It is important to protect your food supply. Which is one reason that so many of us fly far away and fish in the sea for food, as well as eating game. That is another day. Now who will make this kill? Pine you did the last one, so you are out for this one."

"I will," whispered Yew.

"So the rest of you will flush out the deer. Yew will make the kill. That way we will be sure only one is taken. There are no young deer yet, but if you are hunting in the spring, we do not kill mothers. Those with young running with them. We do not leave young ones motherless. It is cruel and it does not assure an increase in your food supply."

They waved their whiplike tails in understanding.

"Remember how I described the fastest way to kill a deer?"

Yew wagged her tail in acknowledgement.

"Now go," Valerian said.

The five wyverns shot into the woods.

"They are doing well," Valerian said, proudly.

"You are a brilliant teacher," Spike said.

"Thank you, and thank you for having such patience as to bring them to our weir. It was the right thing to do. You have good instincts."

"Thank you," he said, bowing his head.

There was a lot of noise in the forest as the deer scattered and ran. Then there was yelling.

Spike instantly went on alert and flew above the forest to see what was happening. This section of the forest was small. On the other side was a clearing. Filled with the Fomorians!

The deer had fled out that side. Choosing to run through the Fomorians rather than hide in the forest with the wyverns streaming through. The wyverns were just about to enter the clearing.

"Help! Fomorians!" sent Spike to any dragon within hearing. The wyverns careened into the clearing, confused by the Fomorians. Spike recognized Balor from previous battles. The giant raised a giant fist, about to hit Bluefire with it.

Spike dove at the giant, claws and teeth ready to rip and tear. Balor's fist came down on Spike's snout. Bluefire must have felt it coming, slipped off to the side. Spike screamed in pain. Snapped at Balor's other arm. Bones crunched between his strong jaws.

Bluefire was back. Biting the giant. Ripping his legs out from under him with her whiplike tail.

The Fomorians with Balor attacked Bluefire. They found themselves flat on the ground from the other wyverns. Yew, Pine and Birch each had two Fomorians trapped with their tails.

"Can I bite this one?" asked Yew.

"Yes, bite Fomorians."

Spike watched as the the wyverns bit and bit and bit. The Fomorians stopped struggling and lay there.

Across the clearing stood another group of Fomorians. They were surrounded by Fae on three sides, several of them riding magnificent horses.

Valerian also stood in front of those Fomorians. Periodically shooting flames at them, just enough to keep their attention.

From down a slope ran several stone warriors. The wyverns looked up.

"Not them," said Spike. "Those are Fae. Our friends."

Above came the flurry of wings and several dragons landed. More hovered in the air above.

Spike looked at Balor and his band. They hadn't moved since the wyverns began biting them. Spike gave a long, slow smile.

In the sunlight his scales shimmered with red. He coughed and a flame shot from his mouth surprising even him.

CHAPTER 46 ~ SOLANGE

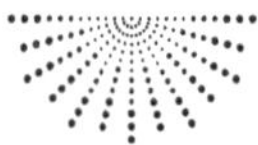

SOLANGE STOOD OFF TO THE SIDE OF THE DRAGON CAVE. Watching most of the Fae climb onto dragons and fly off. She didn't want to be part of this war. She had no skill and even less bravery. Dylan had kissed her and left. Gone to balance out the other elements, as the only water spirit.

Meredith stayed with the other elders, Ogden, Aura, Lea and Conley. They were standing in a circle with three dragons, Silver, Attania and Ethelgarde. The Fae with arms outstretched, touching each other or the dragons. Forming a connection. Then Meredith broke away and came over, grabbing her hand.

"Come, join us. We need your magic."

"I have no magic," said Solange.

"Yes, you do. Otherwise the library wouldn't talk to you. Which she does. She is always leaving books out for you. You have lived in Faerie long enough that your magic is coming in. Just as once we open Faerie again, magic will be loose in the human world. For all of them to access."

Solange followed her. They made a place for her in the circle, Meredith taking one of her hands, Conley with his very warm hand, taking the other. She could actually feel the energy moving around the circle. From touch to touch.

"Ah, that is the energy we were missing," said Aura.

"What do you see now?" asked Attania.

Aura said, "One group of Fomorians, Balor's group, is all down. With wyverns sitting near them. The Fomorians are all bleeding, not moving. As if they were dead. There are dragons and Fae walking everywhere. Checking on them. There are another group of Fomorians. They look like the offspring. They are surrounded by Fae and dragons. Oh, there's Alana and Brian. On horseback. That's why Goshania could not find them at the palace. There really are Fae everywhere. Even the air is filled with sylphs. I cannot tell what is happening with the offspring. Can you ask the pink dragon who is guarding them, Silver?"

"Oh, that would probably be Valerian. She and Spike were teaching the wyverns to hunt today. I'd say they did a fine job."

Silver went silent for a few minutes and then opened her eyes and said, "The Fomorian offspring are trapped, waiting for us to decide what to do with them. They would like to surrender, says one of them. Muir is his name. He appears to be their leader."

Meredith said, "Shall we go down?"

Aura said, "I think we should."

Ethelgarde still wore his rigging from ferrying Fae from the palace. He lay down to make it easier for the elders to climb up.

Solange waited until they were all up and then she climbed up last. She couldn't stay behind if all the elders were going.

"You will be fine, my dear," said Lea, patting Solange's hands after she'd tied herself in. "If there is a problem, you can be sure the Fomorians will not be attacking you or I. They will go for someone who is more powerful."

"You are very powerful," said Solange.

"Me? I am just a simple, earth Fae."

And Ethelgarde took off, diving straight toward the valley.

CHAPTER 47 ~ LEA

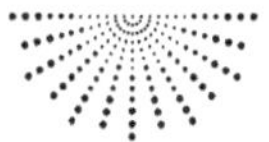

LEA THRILLED TO THE FEELING OF THE AIR WHOOSHING PAST her as the dragon dove. She would have preferred to ride Silver, but her friend wore no rigging.

And Lea was not that brave. Yet.

Perhaps during the summer, the two of them could ride above the meadows of Faerie, taking in all the beauty. Right now there was ugliness to deal with, and death. It was part of the cycle of life and the Fomorians had used up more than their share of living. The ride was short.

Ethelgarde landed in the meadow between the two groups of Fomorians. Solange was the closest to the rope ladder, so she got down first, followed by Lea and the others.

Lea took the human's hand and pulled her off to the side. There were several stone Fae there. Best to stand behind the warriors. They'd be safer.

The field was awful. It was a battleground, after all.

The first group of Fomorians were down, bloody and gnarled. Those small dragons, the wyverns, that's what Aura had called them, looked quite pleased with themselves. They were vicious though.

All the Council stood in a circle now, with Ethelgarde and

Silver. They would decide what to do with the other Fomorians, the offspring.

There must be fifty dragons hovering in the air and hundreds of sylphs. The battlefield was filled with stone, earth and fire Fae. There was the one water spirit, besides Meredith. He stood speaking to some stone warriors. Only water was under represented, most of them still sleeping through the winter.

It was cold down here, but the sun was out, making it awfully bright and Lea had to squint.

The offspring looked anxious. They clearly wanted to run. She could see them still looking for a way out, but those woods were filled with stone and fire Fae and more than a few of the smaller dragons.

She had no doubt if any bolted, that the wyverns would be on them in a flash.

Lea was content to be a bystander. She didn't want to be part of the Council. She did like the idea of spending winters in the palace though. She'd have to figure out spring, summer and fall.

The Council were deep in discussion. They didn't seem to be in agreement. Brian was looking around and then left the circle and walked over to Solange and herself.

"You must come. We need both of your input."

"I'm not an elder," said Solange.

"No, but you are a human. We need a human voice here, and you are an elder Lea. So please come."

There was no arguing with him, Lea knew. She grabbed Solange's hand again and they went over together. And joined the circle. Skin against skin. Lea touched Silver's neck and the beautiful dragon smiled at her.

Meredith said, "So the situation is this. The original Fomorians are dead, as is Plague who had become part of their band. At least as far as we can tell, the wyverns' venom killed them. The wyverns told Spike that they immediately recognized the Fomorians as a threat. They had seen the Fomorians killing wyverns in their minds. I am guessing they have some sort of ancestral memory and the Fomorians and wyverns were mortal enemies."

She continued, "The offspring have surrendered. They wish to go their separate ways and have agreed to leave forever. They never wanted vengeance, they claim. It took them a long time to rebel against Balor. They say they entered Faerie with the wish to tell us they were ending the war against us, and to ask for sanctuary from Balor. To let us know that Balor and the others were weaker. Now that Balor and the others are dead, they would prefer to leave Faerie and never return."

"Do you believe them?" asked Silver. "The Fomorians have not always been forthright with us."

Alana said, "I questioned them. It is difficult to lie to stone Fae. It is possible they are lying, but I cannot see it."

Ethelgarde said, "I think we should have them escorted, one by one, to the edge of Faerie, by a wyvern, a dragon and a group of stone and fire Fae. The others will be guarded by the other wyverns, dragons and Fae, until they are all gone and the boundary fixed so they can never enter again."

Brian said, "That sounds like a good plan. I would add that if they are ever seen by Fae or dragons again, in Faerie or the human world, that they will be killed. We will call the wyverns."

They all agreed and the message was delivered to the Fomorians. Who agreed to the terms. Àed, the volcano was deemed the most dangerous. He left with a group of fire and stone Fae, Spike and a wyvern named Yew. Who snapped at the Fomorian's heels hurrying him along.

Lea sighed with relief. There would be no more beautiful meadows or woods burned by this war.

Silver said to her, "Well, I expect there will be quite the celebration here tonight."

"I expect there will," said Lea. "I hope somebody brought mead."

CHAPTER 48 ~ SKYE

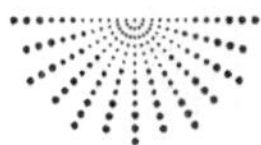

SKYE HOVERED IN THE AIR WITH THE OTHER SYLPHS, UNTIL the final prisoner was escorted to the border of Faerie. The sylphs, along with several dragons followed each and every Fomorian to the boundary and beyond. Àed, the volcano vanished beneath a large mountain in the far north of another country. Muir of the deep, black sea ran to the closest point of land which touched the ocean and dove in. Hurricane blew its way to a different sea and vanished. Lightning left moving far out to the ocean. Blizzard blew north until it left the land and still kept going. Ùisdean of the stone islands, the earthquake, moved far to the west, settling somewhere deep in the Atlantic. The others disappeared as well, some drifting into their elements, others simply fleeing the land as quickly as possible.

The bodies of Balor and the other dead Fomorians were burned in place. No one wanted to touch Plague. Large logs were brought in by the dragons and the heat from the fire could be felt across the meadow.

After all the Fomorians were long gone, most of the sylphs landed and joined the celebration.

Skye wasn't ready to celebrate yet. She flew quickly back to the dragons' caves. It was nearly empty. Attania was there, watching over the hatchlings with a few other caretakers. Skye nodded at them, watching them eat roasted meat. She went down the hallway to check on the hatchling bitten by the wyvern.

Grass and Fern were there, eating as well. And giving some meat to the hatchling.

He was sitting up and when Skye walked in, he wagged his tail against the floor with a thump, thump, thump. The tail was still covered with Dylan's shirt.

"You're okay," she said, surprised.

"He is doing fine," said Fern. "He is tired, but hungry."

Skye put her hands over him. He felt full of energy and his heart was beating strong. She unwrapped the shirt from his tail, removing the poultice. The wound looked clean and the puncture marks had healed over.

"I think we can take this off. Just watch out to make sure it doesn't become inflamed again. If it turns red, then call me back and I'll see what else I can do."

"We cannot thank you enough," said Grass.

"I was pleased to be able to help. That is what healers do, is it not?" said Skye.

"Yes, it is," said Fern. "Please return on a day when things are calmer, so you can speak to us of Fae healing."

"Yes, we would like to learn more," said Grass.

"I think I will," said Skye. "Another day, then."

She ran down the tunnel, waved at the caretakers and hatchlings, then dove off the cliff, soaring back down to the valley.

Night had fallen since she'd left. A beautiful full moon was rising, still so low in the sky it looked huge and orange.

Skye returned to the celebration, her heart soaring with happiness.

She found Aidan and shared his mug of mead, and his warmth. She was never going to let him go again.

From somewhere, probably the palace, roasted meat and other food had been flown in by the dragons. Mead and other wine arrived. Smaller fires were built. All of Faerie seemed to be here celebrating tonight.

Across one fire, Skye caught sight of Egan and Lassair, kissing. She smiled, pleased that they had worked things out.

A dance began and she ran into Dylan, pulling him and Solange aside, telling them the tale of his lost shirt and how it saved a baby dragon's life.

"I will have to go visit him," Dylan said, smiling.

"What will you do with your art now?" asked Skye.

"I don't know. Just paint, probably. Get back in touch with my agent. Come out as Fae. Try to do my part in acclimating the human world to Faerie."

In the middle of the celebration, Ogden called for everyone's attention.

He said, his resonant voice sounding across the valley, "This is a momentous occasion. With the demise of the Fomorians, the Council of Luminaries has decided that there is no longer any need for the boundary surrounding Faerie. We therefore open Faerie to the world, once again. We will begin the process of gently letting humans know that we exist, but that will be tomorrow. Because tonight, we celebrate."

And with that, Skye looked up to see the boundary covering Faerie disintegrate into thin air. Sparks flew and lightening crackled. Then it looked as if it had never been with the clear starlit sky shimmering above.

Aidan squeezed her tightly, kissing her forehead.

She saw a dragon take off, carrying one single rider. Ethelgarde, with his opalescent scales, gleamed like a rainbow in the moonlight, his colors flashing. His massive wings pounded the air until he rose high above the trees and sped off to the east.

Skye smiled, knowing where Ethelgarde was flying. He was taking Fiachna to Clare.

She felt as if her heart would burst with joy for those around her. And for herself. She would be going back to do what she loved, healing others. With the one she loved.

Faerie was safe.

* * *

IF YOU'VE READ THE ENTIRE SERIES, PLEASE CONSIDER leaving a review for the books. Even a short review is greatly appreciated. Reviews help other readers find books they might love.

Click on the links below and it should take you to a page where you can leave one. Thank you so much!

Faerie Unraveled: The Bones of the Earth Series, Book 1

Faerie Contact: The Bones of the Earth, Book 2

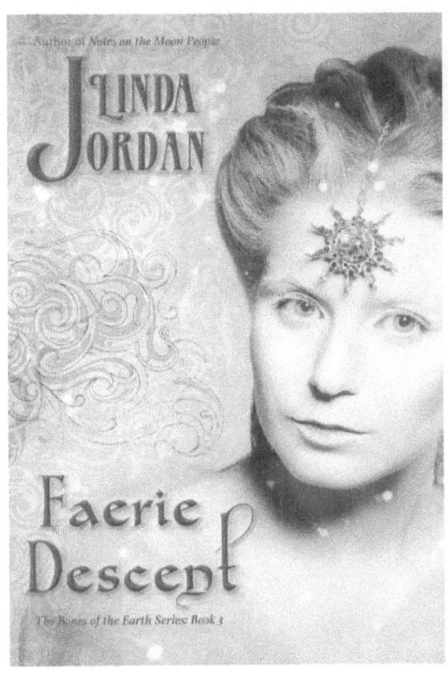

Faerie Descent: The Bones of the Earth, Book 3

Faerie Flight: The Bones of the Earth, Book 4

Faerie Confluence: The Bones of the Earth, Book 5

ABOUT THE AUTHOR

Linda Jordan writes fascinating characters, visionary worlds, and imaginative fiction. She creates both long and short fiction, serious and silly. She believes in the power of healing and transformation, and many of her stories follow those themes.
In a previous lifetime, Linda coordinated the Clarion West Writers' Workshop as well as the Reading Series. She spent four years as Chair of the Board of Directors during Clarion West's formative period. She's also worked as a travel agent, a baker, and a pond plant/fish sales person, you know, the sort of things one does as a writer.
Currently, she's the Programming Director for the Writers Cooperative of the Pacific Northwest.
Linda now lives in the rainy wilds of Washington state with her husband, daughter, four cats, a cluster of Koi and an infinite number of slugs and snails.

Her other work includes:
~Faerie Unraveled: The Bones of the Earth: Book 1
~Faerie Contact: The Bones of the Earth: Book 2
~Faerie Descent: The Bones of the Earth: Book 3
~Faerie Flight: The Bones of the Earth: Book 4
~Faerie Confluence: The Bones of the Earth: Book 5
~Rescue Mission: Islands of Seattle: Book 1
~Explosive Resistance: Islands of Seattle: Book 2
~Battle Magic: Islands of Seattle: Book 3
~Warriors Rising: Islands of Seattle: Book 4

~Divine War: Islands of Seattle: Book 5
~Infected by Magic
~Notes on the Moon People
~Falling Into Flight
~The Black Opal: Jeweled Worlds Series: Book 1
~The Enigmatic Pearl: Jeweled Worlds Series: Book 2
~The Flaming Ruby: Jeweled Worlds Series: Book 3

All her work can be found at your favorite online bookseller.

Get a FREE ebook!
Sign up for Linda's Serendipitous Newsletter at her website:
www.LindaJordan.net

Visit her at: www.LindaJordan.net
She can be found on Facebook at:
www.facebook.com/LindaJordanWriter

Metamorphosis Press website is at: www.MetamorphosisPress.com

Writers love reviews, even short, simple ones and honest reviews help other readers find the book. Please go to where you bought this book, or Goodreads, and leave a review. It would be much appreciated.